THE SECRET AGENTS
STRIKE BACK

THE SECRET AGENTS

STRIKE BACK

Robyn Freedman Spizman
& Mark Johnston

ATHENEUM BOOKS FOR YOUNG READERS
New York   London   Toronto   Sydney

Atheneum Books for Young Readers
An imprint of Simon & Schuster Children's Publishing Division
1230 Avenue of the Americas
New York, New York 10020

Book design by Krista Vossen
The text for this book is set in Garth Graphic.
Manufactured in the United States of America
First Edition
10 9 8 7 6 5 4 3 2 1
Library of Congress Cataloging-in-Publication Data
Spizman, Robyn Freedman.
The secret agents strike back / Robyn Freedman Spizman and
Mark Johnston.—1st ed.
p. cm.
Sequel to: Secret agent.
Summary: High schooler Kyle and his "secret agent" friends
uncover a medical mystery when they embark on a mission to
prevent fellow "agent" (and Kyle's secret crush) Lucinda from
moving away from New York City.
ISBN-13: 978-1-4169-0086-3
ISBN-10: 1-4169-0086-1
[1. Friendship—Fiction. 2. Swindlers and swindling—Fiction.
3. New York (N.Y.)—Fiction.] I. Johnston, Mark, 1948–
II. Title.
PZ7.S7595Si 2007
[Fic]—dc22
2006024430

ACKNOWLEDGMENTS

My deepest thanks to my husband, Willy, and our children, Justin and Ali, whose endless affection and love sustain me. To my devoted parents, Jack and Phyllis Freedman, who have always said I could do anything I put my mind to. To my brother, Doug, who believed in *Secret Agent* when it was just an idea, and to Doug's real life Genie, Dr. Sam and Gena Spizman, Lois Blonder, Ramona Freedman, and the rest of my beloved family and friends (you know who you are!). My heartfelt thanks to Betty Storne, our real-life angel: You are one of life's truest treasures. And a special thanks to my talented coauthor Mark Johnston. You are a true credit to the literary world! —R. S.

Thanks to my coauthor, Robyn Freedman Spizman, for changing my life. Thanks to Scott Parker, not only for knowing his stuff but also for explaining it with such patience and humor. Thanks to Andy Chansen, even though the law he researched didn't make the final edit. Thanks to Philip Whitley for letting me steal his onomatopoeia. Thanks to my family—the Johnstons, the Georges, the Hesses, and the Cyrs (especially Art and the late Audrey Cyr for passing along such wonderful genes). And thanks to Mark Davis for long ago showing me how much words count. —M. J.

Thank you again to our agents, Mary Lee and Ron Laitsch, for believing in the secret agents and for all your support through all these years. Thank you to Emily Crehan and Alison Velea for your close reads. Thank you to Krista Vossen for the great design and to Tim Jessell for an illustration that leaps off the jacket. And thank you to our editor, Susan Burke, for all the hours and all the encouragement and for being such a pro. We sure were lucky when our manuscript arrived in your hands. —R. S. and M. J.

CHAPTER 1

The moon was a sliver.

There was no light, not on Twentieth Street in New York City that Thursday, April 19, at ten minutes past midnight. It wasn't the darkness, however, that made Lucinda Winston slip out of bed and tiptoe to her door. It was her parents. They were whispering. But it was the kind of whispering you can hear all the way down the hall and into your bedroom.

"I'm sorry!" her mom said. "I can't work there any longer! I just can't!"

"So quit!" Lucinda's dad said.

"I have! I mean, I will!" Lucinda's mom said. "I've already accepted a job at Emory University!"

"In Atlanta?" Lucinda's dad said. "You've accepted a job in Atlanta, Georgia, without discussing it with Lucinda and me?"

"I said I'm sorry!"

"Sorry doesn't cut it!"

"Keep your voice down!" Lucinda's mom said. "We don't want to wake Lucinda!"

But Lucinda was already awake. She'd been rereading

Pride and Prejudice under her quilt when she heard the fear in her mom's voice and slipped out from under the covers. And, no, Lucinda had never spied on her parents before. But Lucinda had never heard her parents argue before. Well, that wasn't true. But the arguments had always been about her dad dumping his dirty clothes in the closet or her mom interrupting a baseball game on TV, not moving to another city in another state and leaving New York City forever!

The house was silent.

Dead silent.

But Lucinda knew her father wasn't finished. She knew he was building up to something. Lucinda could feel it all the way down the hall and through her door, and there was nothing she could do about it but wait and listen until her dad finally said:

"Don't you think it's time you stopped hiding?"

I swear.

Those were the exact words Lucinda's dad said to her mom. *"Don't you think it's time you stopped hiding?"* A blast of hot air shot into Lucinda's windpipe. She tried to swallow, but the air stuck there, refusing to seep into her lungs. She wanted to jump back under the covers and stare at the stars her mother had painted on the ceiling when Lucinda was five years old. But Lucinda knew the stars wouldn't keep her father's words from tingling up her backbone. No, not tingling. Digging their claws in and not letting go. All Lucinda could imagine was her mom trying to escape from some shadowy man in a long leather coat with a scar on his cheek and a dagger strapped to his ankle. Which was silly, of course. But you always imagine the worst. Or, at least, Lucinda did. Or, at least, she did that night in that pitch-black darkness. And that was before she heard her mom whisper:

"But I have no proof!"

2

Lucinda's brownstone was on Twentieth Street between Eighth and Ninth Avenues in Chelsea just above the meat-packing district on the west side of Manhattan. Yeah, I know. *Just above the meat-packing district* doesn't sound like a place I'd like to live either. But the meat-packing plants were long gone, and Chelsea was now way hip with its specialty gourmet shops and trendy restaurants which, I assure you, were as big a yawn to Lucinda as they are to you.

But, still, Chelsea was in New York.

And Lucinda loved New York.

Not just the museums and the Broadway plays and the screaming subways shooting through those deep, dark, underground tunnels and the guys on the street corners selling roasted chestnuts the moment the temperature dropped below forty degrees. Sure, that was cool, as cool as Times Square lit up every night like the Fourth of July. But Lucinda didn't just love the fun stuff. She loved the mobbed sidewalks and the bumper-to-bumper traffic and the wrecking balls smashing down buildings so bigger buildings could be put up in their place. She loved the taxi drivers tossing change back at the feet of the riders who didn't tip enough and the smell of horse sweat when you got too close to the buggies clip-clopping around Central Park.

But you know what?

That was all background noise. If Lucinda were really being honest, she wouldn't say she loved New York because of the fun stuff *or* the crazy stuff. Lucinda Winston loved living in New York because of one reason and one reason only. Because Kyle Parker lived across the street. Because he'd always lived across the street. And she especially loved it since the afternoon at the concrete park when Kyle had asked her to become a secret agent.

Maybe you've heard of Kyle Parker.

Maybe not.

He was this skinny-armed kid with a cowlick. Nothing special to look at. Not really. Not unless you caught that spark of brilliance behind those pale blue eyes. I'm not saying Kyle was school-smart. He wasn't a straight-A student like Lucinda. It was more the *way* Kyle thought. He could work things out you didn't think could get worked out. Take the secret agents. He'd started them because of *Love in Autumn*. That was the book his dad had been writing for six years. Kyle started the secret agents to get *Love in Autumn* published, even though his dad hadn't been able to do it for six long years.

Impossible?

Not to Kyle.

Sure, the odds were like a zillion to one. But that didn't stop Kyle from getting Lucinda to help him swipe a copy of *Love in Autumn*, slip past the security guard at Boykin Books, and set up the most elaborate bait-and-switch operation ever attempted by a pack of kids inside a swank restaurant on Central Park South, all to

4

catch the eye of Mercedes Henderson (the most famous editor at Boykin Books).

And it had worked.

It all worked.

Mercedes Henderson loved the book, *Love in Autumn* shot up the bestseller charts, and the next thing the secret agents knew the Sunday *Style* section of the *New York Times* was running a feature article on "The Kids with the Golden Touch." And that was just the beginning. The secret agents' second submission to Boykin Books—*Any Idiot Can Clean a House*—hit number three on amazon.com, and four months later Mercedes Henderson was on the *Late Show with David Letterman* plugging the secret agents' *third* discovery, *The Goofy Animal Alphabet Book* by Lisa Boatwright:

> *A is for Antelope*
> *who love to eat cantaloupe.*
> *B is for Bats*
> *who look silly in hats . . .*

But fame is tricky. So is taste. Even with all the positive buzz and publicity, *The Goofy Animal Alphabet Book* was a flop. No one bought it. Okay, okay. So the secret agents' parents bought it. But no *kids* bought it. Kids *hated* it. They didn't think the pictures of antelopes holding cantaloupes in their hooves were funny. They didn't think bats in backward baseball caps with baggy jeans slung way down on their tiny legs were funny. Which went double for Harry R. Boykin, the president and publisher of Boykin Books. He didn't think anything about *The Goofy Animal Alphabet Book* was funny. His company lost a ton of money. All because of Kyle Parker and the secret agents. Or, at least, that was who Harry R. Boykin blamed. Because somebody had to be blamed. And the secret agents were the ones who brought the manuscript to Boykin Books in the first place. And weren't they the ones with the *golden touch?*

So it went.

On and on.

With one exception: Mercedes Henderson. She never blamed Kyle. She never blamed the secret agents. She sucked it up. She took the heat. She never once pointed the finger at anyone other than herself.

"You take chances," Mercedes Henderson told a *Newsweek* reporter. "That's what editors do. That's what *I* do. *The Goofy Animal Alphabet Book* didn't sell. That's too bad. But I'm the one who made the decision to publish it."

Tough?

Gutsy?

You bet. Good for Mercedes Henderson! Way to go, Mercedes Henderson! Though, when it came right down to it, it didn't really matter what Mercedes Henderson said. Not to Kyle. The book was still a flop. Which made Kyle feel like a flop. And, yeah, I know. It doesn't necessarily follow that one false move turns someone into a flop.

But you haven't heard the whole story yet.

You haven't heard Chad.

Not that I expect you to recognize his name either. If you don't know Kyle Parker, you certainly don't know Chad Simon—obnoxious Chad Simon, self-centered Chad Simon.

Wait a minute!

Don't play that game with me!

Don't you be thinking:

Why should I care about Kyle Parker when he was such a wuss that he listened to an obnoxious, self-centered jerk?

Like you don't have any obnoxious friends? Like no one you hang out with is self-centered? Chad was Kyle's oldest friend. They'd known each other since first grade. And Chad had always been loyal. Which meant Kyle had always been loyal. I'm not saying it was easy. I'm not saying there weren't times when Chad didn't push the bonds of that loyalty. Take the last secret agent meeting, for instance—the one right after *The Goofy Animal Alphabet Book* had become such an embarrassment.

"See?" Chad cried. "The book stinks! I always said it stinks!"

"No, you didn't!" Ruben said.

"Maybe not!" Chad said. "But I always *thought* it!"

Ruben said nothing. Ruben gave Chad a look. But the look was enough. Chad may have been obnoxious, but he wasn't crazy. He wasn't about to face off with Ruben. Because Ruben was Ruben Gomez—the greatest high school basketball player in New York City. We're talking huge. College coaches lining up around the block. A possible jump straight into the NBA.

Okay.

Okay.

I know what you're thinking: What was a jock like Ruben doing hanging out with a pack of bookworms?

Answer:

Lucinda.

Ruben liked Lucinda. And he didn't mind showing it. Ever since school started back up in September, he'd been putting a full court press on her like you wouldn't believe—sending her flowers, hanging out with her between classes, carrying her backpack to and from school, taking her home to meet his mom. Name a mushy-gushy, cornball cliché, and Ruben was all over it. Like syrup on a sundae. Mr. Big-Shot Athlete with the heart of a marshmallow.

As you might imagine, this was okay with Lucinda. Though it didn't mean she wasn't confused. Of course she was confused. Last year she was this nerdy little eighth grader still stuck in PS 126, and this year Ruben Gomez was trailing her around Roosevelt High like a lap dog. And, yeah, she'd always had a crush on Kyle, but where were *his* flowers? Why didn't *he* offer to carry her backpack to school? And come on! We're talking Ruben Gomez here! Can you imagine what it was like walking down the hallway with the most popular kid in school? The girls wanted to be her. The boys wanted to date her.

All the boys.

Except one.

Kyle Parker.

Or maybe he did. Maybe he'd just stopped talking to her because he was jealous of Ruben. Lucinda wasn't sure. But she was sure of the exact moment that everything changed.

Six days ago.

Friday the thirteenth.

Lucinda had never been superstitious, so her guard hadn't been up when Kyle arrived on her front steps with this lost look in his eyes grumbling about some unnamed, online Barnes and Noble reviewer giving *The Goofy Animal Alphabet Book* half a star and calling the secret agents "a bunch of punk kids who may have struck lightning with *Love in Autumn* and *Any Idiot Can Clean a House* but who were obviously illiterate lucky stiffs."

Lucinda's response?

A shrug.

Not that she didn't care about the book. She just thought Kyle was being a little too dramatic. "Who cares about some stupid review by some stupid reviewer who doesn't even have the guts to sign his name?" That was what her shrug was supposed to mean. It was supposed to cheer Kyle up and snap him out of it. But right then—before Lucinda had a chance to explain—her father opened the front door and said Ruben was on the phone to tell her what time he'd pick her up for dinner.

And that was it.

Kyle's lost look turned to stone. He knew about Lucinda and Ruben, of course. But the timing of Ruben's call right at that exact moment was more than Kyle could take. He didn't nod. He didn't say good-bye. He stomped down the steps and raced across the street before she had a chance to explain. That was six days ago. And he hadn't said a word to her since.

But he would now.

He'd have to.

Lucinda wasn't going to give him a choice. Because there wasn't any way she could go to her parents. The tone of their whispers had made it clear that asking either one of them why her mom was hiding wasn't an option. But that didn't mean Lucinda wasn't going to try to find out.

Not by herself.

Not when Kyle Parker lived right across the street.

And, yeah, up to this point, the secret agents had only gone undercover to get *Love in Autumn* published. But that was about to change. Lucinda was going to make sure it changed. Or this time next month she might be living in Atlanta. And her mom would still be hiding.

Without any proof!

CHAPTER 3

"Proof of what?"

Chad said this. He said it rolling his eyes toward the ceiling as the secret agents sat cross-legged in a circle in Kyle's dad's old office on the ground floor of Kyle's brownstone at 5:15 the next morning. That's right. 5:15. Lucinda had tossed and turned all night, repeating her mom and dad's conversation over and over and over until she finally heard the Chelsea Newsstand guy on Eighth Avenue roll up the metal curtain in front of the newsstand.

And that was it.

That was all she could take.

She speed-dialed Kyle's cell phone and woke him up and told him she couldn't wait until Saturday to meet at the Tofu Tutti-Frutti where the secret agents always met every Saturday morning. So Kyle crawled out of bed and speed-dialed Chad, Tyrone, and Ruben, and twenty minutes later they all sat cross-legged in a circle, yawning and shivering on the hardwood floor of Kyle's dad's empty office. Even though it looked out on the back patio garden and had the best view in Kyle's house,

10

the room had no desk, no desk chair, no bookcase, no books. Creepy? You bet it was creepy in that chilly, early-morning air, especially since it was still pitch-black outside and the only light was a candle flickering in the center of their circle, causing Chad's shadow to dance on the wall behind him as he said "Proof of what?" in a whisper so obnoxious it made Tyrone want to grab Chad by the collar and shake him.

"Why don't you look at Lucinda when you talk to her?" Tyrone said.

"Who said I was talking to her, *Opera Boy?*" Chad said.

"Don't call me Opera Boy," Tyrone said. "And since Lucinda was the only one in the room who just said her mom had no proof, who else could you be talking to?"

So okay.

So you've already met Chad. But Tyrone Brown was a different story altogether. He was a secret agent, of course. He was also a friend of Kyle's. But Tyrone's relationship with Chad was a bit more complicated. You see, Tyrone hadn't been around back in first grade. Tyrone hadn't known Kyle when he moved to Twentieth Street and needed a friend. So Tyrone didn't really see the point of Chad Simon at all. In fact, Tyrone and Chad wouldn't have hung out in the same room together—and they certainly wouldn't have been secret agents together—if it hadn't been for Kyle. They put up with each other so they could be friends with Kyle. But that didn't mean they cut each other any slack. Take the Opera Boy slam. There was nothing Chad liked better than slipping that one in every chance he got.

Why?

Because it worked.

Tyrone hated it. Mostly because it was true. Tyrone

was an opera boy. He *loved* opera. More than that, he *sang* opera. Plus, Tyrone was shy and insecure. Which wouldn't have been all that big a deal if Tyrone had been a jock like Ruben or a brainiac like Lucinda. You know, the usual. Every high school has at least half a dozen, along with a pack of computer geeks and a squad of cheerleaders. But a boy who sang opera? I don't think so. Even kids in the band weren't all that sure what to say to the only kid in the history of Roosevelt High who took a master class in voice at the Julliard School of Music three days a week.

Chad?

The flip side. A hundred and eighty degrees. Chad was *too* sure of himself. He never shut up. Plus, his favorite topic always centered around the pile of money he'd be making as a future plastic surgeon by sucking the blubber out of your belly or breaking your nose then putting it back together again. Or maybe I should say it always *had been* his favorite topic. Because it no longer was. Because the moment the secret agents made their one and only headline, Chad immediately switched to a new favorite topic. Though it still certainly centered all around him.

"I'm just saying," Chad said, "that as a secret agent— which is what I am, a secret agent—I'm just saying I want to know. Lucinda heard her mom say she has no proof. So, as a secret agent, I just want to know what proof Lucinda's mom was talking about."

"Duh!" Tyrone said.

"What's that supposed to mean?" Chad said.

"It *means*," Ruben said, "that we'd all like to know what proof Lucinda's mom was talking about."

"She's scared," Lucinda said. "I could hear it in her voice."

"Maybe she's hiding out from someone," Chad said.

12

"Can't be," Ruben said. "Her name's in the phone book."

"Maybe she's changed her name," Chad said. "Maybe she's a crook. Maybe she's on the run with the cops on her tail."

"Shut up!" Lucinda said.

"Wait a minute! Wait a minute!" Tyrone said. "Maybe she *is* on the run! But maybe it isn't the police who are after her!"

Silence.

Total.

From the secret agents, I mean. Not from the outside world. Because at that very moment, the wind began to whistle through the cracks in the window. The panes rattled. The wood around the glass shook. It was like nature's way of showing Lucinda what was going on inside herself. That shadowy man in the long leather coat with the knife strapped to his ankle? He was back. Back in her imagination. Tyrone's words had brought him back. Because if someone else was thinking the same thing she'd been thinking, then maybe her thoughts hadn't been so silly after all.

"Now what?"

This was Chad. He asked the question, though it could just as easily have been Lucinda or Ruben or Tyrone. Not Kyle. Never Kyle. He was the one the other four would have been asking. From the moment the secret agents first began, Kyle had been the leader. He was the one with the big ideas. He was the one who would save the day.

Lucinda's mom was hiding?

She didn't have any proof?

No sweat.

Kyle would solve it. Kyle would come up with the plan. Not a single member of those secret agents sitting crossed-legged around that burning candle doubted it for a second.

But as I've already told you, the flop of *The Goofy Animal Alphabet Book* plus Chad rubbing it in plus Ruben liking Lucinda (and Lucinda acting as if she liked Ruben back) had all taken their toll. Especially over the past six days. Ever since Kyle had marched off in a huff from Lucinda's front doorstep, he'd lost that spark in his eyes. He couldn't sleep. He couldn't eat. Heck, he hadn't even told Chad to shut up five minutes ago when Chad deserved to be told to shut up.

In other words, the other secret agents may have looked up to Kyle, but Kyle no longer looked up to himself. He no longer believed in himself. Sure, he'd called the secret agent meeting. Sure, he'd heard everything that was said and knew they were now all staring at him, waiting to hear what their next move should be. But Kyle had no next move. He was so shook up that Lucinda's mom was making Lucinda move to Atlanta that his jaw locked and his tongue practically drew blood when it rubbed across the roof of his mouth.

So Kyle said nothing.

Kyle shrugged.

It was the stupidest thing he'd ever done in his life. Why? Because, as you might imagine, Lucinda saw it as payback for six days ago when she'd shrugged at him.

"Wait!" Kyle said.

Too late.

Lucinda had already snuffed out the candle and raced out the door.

CHAPTER 4

Who was the first person Kyle told about the secret agents? Who picked the lock to his dad's desk? Who discovered Mercedes Henderson was the perfect editor for *Love in Autumn*? Who gave Kyle the guts to sneak past the Boykin Books security guard?

Lucinda.

It was always Lucinda.

Which led to the last question—the big question: *What were the secret agents without Lucinda?* And the more Kyle asked himself this question, the more the answer made him feel as empty as his dad's empty office.

So okay.

So you want to know why.

Not why Kyle was feeling empty. You already know the answer to that. But you might not know that Kyle's mom and dad had split. Not divorced. They were separated. Walter Parker lived fifteen blocks away on Greenwich Avenue above the Open Book even after *Love in Autumn* started selling like wildfire and Walter Parker could have moved to plenty of other places. But a real apartment would have seemed so permanent. Like his old life was over. Like he was giving up. So, as far as Kyle's dad was concerned, it was simple: He still lived where he lived because he hoped that one day he might move back to Twentieth Street. Same with Kyle's mom. Polly Parker hadn't turned Kyle's dad's old, empty office into a library or a TV room yet because she figured as long as it stayed empty, there was always the chance that Kyle's dad's desk and office chair might one day fill it up again.

Though it wasn't going to happen any day soon.

Because Kyle's dad was out in Los Angeles working on the screenplay to *Love in Autumn*. Which meant if Kyle wanted any face-to-face fatherly advice on what to do about Lucinda, he'd have to wait at least two months. Not that they didn't talk on the phone every other day. But talking wasn't seeing. Plus, it just seemed weird asking his dad about girls. First off, it was embarrassing. And, second off, what could his dad tell him? After all, he didn't seem to be doing all that hot with Kyle's mom.

So who did Kyle turn to?

Shakespeare.

Not the dead guy your English teachers are always talking about. The dog. Shakespeare was a dog. And not even Kyle's dog. Shakespeare belonged to Percy Percerville, who lived in the townhouse right next door to Lucinda. A year ago, Percy hired Kyle to walk Shakespeare every morning and afternoon for money. Though Kyle would have walked Shakespeare for nothing. Because Kyle loved Shakespeare. Even though Shakespeare was nuts.

Yeah, I know.

How can a dog be nuts?

A dog is just a dog.

Unless he cuddles up against you one minute and runs yowling away the next. Not because you hit him or yell at him. But because that was what Shakespeare did. The same way he pretended that any man standing still was a fire hydrant and any baby was a Frisbee. And, no, he never locked his jaw onto a six-month-old and sent her twirling across the street. But one glimpse of a stroller, and Shakespeare leaped up on his hind legs, teeth at the ready, drool pouring out of his mouth. Suffice it to say there weren't a whole lot of men leaning against buildings or women pushing newborns in the early mornings or late afternoons anywhere near Twentieth Street when Kyle took Shakespeare for his walk.

Nor was there ever a huge crowd hanging out too close to the seesaw in the concrete park on Twenty-first Street and Ninth Avenue, where Kyle and Shakespeare always stopped to chat. Which was what they were doing at 6:17 that very same morning, less than thirty minutes after Ruben, Chad, and Tyrone had followed Lucinda out of that empty office to get ready for school.

Kyle was sitting on the seesaw. Shakespeare was sitting on the concrete next to the seesaw. The two of them were chatting. Or, at least, Kyle was. While Shakespeare licked himself. Then licked Kyle. Who, as you might imagine, needed all the licks he could get.

"She's leaving, Shakespeare!" Kyle said. "Lucinda's mom is making Lucinda move to Atlanta! What can I do, Shakespeare? How can I stop her? I can't change Lucinda's mom's mind! And even if I could, why should I? Lucinda likes Ruben. Not me! Ruben!"

Shakespeare didn't answer.

He didn't bark or growl or whimper. He just licked Kyle. Which really didn't count as an answer. Though it was nice. Kyle liked it. And who knows how long he would have gone on liking it if Percy Percerville's booming baritone hadn't jolted Kyle out of his trance.

"No, dear boy!" Percy exclaimed. "*Walking* a dog does not mean *sitting* a dog! It means motion! Forward motion! Perambulation, as it were! Heel-to-toe! Heel-to-toe! Heel-to-toe!"

You think Shakespeare was nuts?

Well, check out his master:

Outside of circus tents and Saturday-morning cartoons, Percy Percerville was the only human being—male or female—that Kyle had ever seen who wore red (all red) shirts, socks, suits, and ties under a black cape (with red lining) and carried a walking stick—a gold-tipped walking stick—which, at that very moment, he happened to be tapping on the concrete to emphasize his point.

"Exercise!" Percy declared. "It unclogs the arteries, clears the head, and flushes the toxins through the pores of the skin. I should know. I never partake in the activity. And neither, I now discover, does my dog."

"Have you been spying on us?" Kyle said.

"*Spying* is such an ugly word. I circumnavigated the block at a discreet interval behind your and Shakespeare's forlorn footfalls. And who can blame me? Ever since I first peeked through my third-story curtains six days ago and astutely ascertained that a certain basketball phenomenon had begun popping up every morning before school to escort the lovely Lucinda to Roosevelt High, I've come to notice that you, dear boy, have been mooning about the neighborhood in such a hangdog state that I would have been derelict in my duties if I hadn't taken it upon myself to delve into the matter more deeply."

Whoa!

Stop!

Back it up a moment. Because this was big. Humongous. Percy Percerville never delved into any matter (mooning or otherwise). Not during working hours. Which, as far as Percy was concerned, began at six a.m. and often continued well past midnight. And even if he did spot something out of the ordinary, he never actually left his house to check it out.

Because Percy had a secret.

He was Cynthia Marlow, the biggest selling romance novelist of all time. Cynthia Marlow was the fake name Percy used when he wrote his two novels a year, every year, for the last seventeen years in a row. Why did he hire Kyle? So Percy could seclude himself inside his four-story townhouse and write and write and write without having to worry about interacting with the world in general or pooper-scoopers in particular. Which was the reason this moment was so big. A first! Oh, sure, Kyle and Percy had talked before. And Percy had even been helpful (in his convoluted fashion), but only when Kyle had interrupted Percy. Not the other way around. Never the other way around. Until this very moment. Right here. Right now.

"Duties?" Kyle said.

"As your employer, dear boy. The payer of your meager salary. The guardian of your capitalist soul."

"You don't think I earn my salary?"

"I think you're upset. Which upsets Shakespeare. Which upsets me. And I can't be upset. It breaks the razor-thin edge of my Zen-like concentration. In short, dear boy, there can be no weak links in my organizational chain."

"You're calling me weak?"

"Next to Ruben? Yes, dear boy, I'm afraid I am."

Whoa!

Stop again!

Shortly after he started walking Shakespeare, Kyle discovered Percy's secret. And, yeah, Kyle told Lucinda. He couldn't stop himself from telling Lucinda. But that was it. She was all he told. Kyle's dad found out later but not because Kyle or Lucinda blabbed. They never did. Not to anyone. Even though a national tabloid offered a $10,000 reward to anyone who would. Which was why Kyle thought Percy respected him. Liked him, even. Or, at least, Kyle figured Percy wouldn't go out of his way to find Kyle's weak spot and rub it in.

"Ah!" Percy said. "You find my last statement indelicate. Mean-spirited. Hard-hearted to the max. And maybe it was, dear boy. Maybe it was. But before you castigate me completely and slink off to wallow in your teenage self-pity, focus on the following facts. *A:* Are you not now faced with a dilemma, a dilemma that has all but fractured your adolescent heart? *B:* Am I not the author of romance novels, novels that, by definition, deal *exclusively* with matters of the heart? *C:* Put those two facts together, and who would you say is the one more abused? The prideful child who seeks no advice? Or the humble, soft-spoken expert who only wishes to pass along his proven expertise?"

"You want to help me with Lucinda?" Kyle said.

"Ask Shakespeare, dear boy. As you can see, he's wagging his tail."

5

Parents are people.

Yeah, I know. Obvious. But stick with me a moment. We all remember a time when our mom could make a scraped knee stop stinging by kissing our tears away and our dad could throw a football farther than anyone alive. We might even remember the exact moment it finally dawned on us that our mom's kisses were simply a distraction, and our Dad's right arm wasn't getting him any signing bonus to the NFL.

Ditto Lucinda.

As far as her dad was concerned, at least.

I'm not saying she suddenly figured out her dad was a dolt. Just human. A guy who designed neon lights for a living and a pretty good living at that. But her mom . . . Well, for starters, Lucinda's mom just happened to be this big deal molecular biology professor at NYU who spent all her working hours trying to stop outlaw cells from causing cancer. And, the way Lucinda saw it, if anyone could stop those cells, it was her mom. You see, Lucinda was a reader. She read everything she could get her hands on and remembered everything she ever read. No matter. She couldn't stump her mom. Whatever factoid Lucinda had plucked out of that day's book or magazine article, Lucinda's mom could always fill in the blank.

Not that she rubbed it in.

Professor Winston never tried to show her daughter who was who. In fact, there were times Lucinda caught her mom pretending *not* to know how to find the area of an isosceles triangle or which course had the longest Par 5 on the PGA tour. In other words, Lucinda's mom had always been so confident she didn't have to prove she was confident. She let other people shine. She let her daughter shine. Or so Lucinda had always thought.

But maybe she had it wrong. Maybe her mom didn't grab the spotlight because she was hiding. Maybe she'd always been hiding. Did that mean Lucinda was hiding too? Now? Was that why she hadn't said anything to Kyle when he'd shrugged but went running out the door and kept running all the way across the street and into her house where she collapsed onto her living room couch and burst out crying?

I'm not talking about a tear trickling down her cheek or the sniffles. I'm saying Lucinda wrapped her arms around herself and exploded. Her shoulders shook. She curled herself into a ball. Slobber and spit shot out of her mouth so loud she woke her mom, who came racing down the stairs so fast she forgot to tie her bathrobe and nearly tripped over the belt.

"Lucinda? Dear? What's wrong? What is it?"

Lucinda didn't answer.

Not right away.

It wasn't that she *couldn't* answer. Her larynx wasn't shut down. Unlike her brain. Which was locked on her mom's hanging bathrobe belt. And that was it. That was when the knot inside Lucinda finally unraveled, and she suddenly realized her mom wasn't this perfect superhero but a living, breathing person who had faults like everybody else.

"Why do we have to leave New York?" Lucinda shouted. "Why are you making us move to Atlanta?"

"How did you find out?" Lucinda's mom said.

Which wasn't an answer. Which wasn't even close to an answer. But even worse were Lucinda's mom's eyes. Not that they blinked or wandered around the room. They simply shut down. As if a curtain had been dropped. A steel curtain. A curtain Lucinda had never seen before.

"Last night I wasn't asleep," Lucinda said. "I could hear you and dad talking all the way down the hall."

"Oh."

"*Oh* doesn't cut it!"

"Who do you think you're talking to?" Lucinda's mom said.

"Mom! This is our home! It's *my* home! What if *I* don't want to move?"

"Lucinda. Sweetheart. There are some things you don't understand."

"So explain them! What are you so afraid of? Your job? You love your job! Your boss? Crazy old John T. Beecham? Has he cracked up something more than just his hip?"

"Lucinda!"

"I'm sorry, Mom! I know you like him! And I know he's in the hospital! And I know I should be nice to him even though he's always eating those icky root beer candies! But, Mom! Please! Tell me why we have to move!"

"I can't."

"Yes, you can! We're talking about New York! The city you've lived in from the time you were my age!

Grandpa's pharmacy was on Fourteenth Street! You went to Roosevelt High too! You always said it made you so happy that I'd graduate from the same high school where you graduated! And now we're moving? Just like that? You have to tell me why!"

But nothing.

No go.

The steel curtain was clamped down tight.

CHAPTER 6

After school that afternoon Kyle saw the FOR SALE sign inside Lucinda's living-room window. He saw it on his way to pick up Shakespeare, and his stomach twisted itself into a tourniquet. I'm not saying his whole body hadn't already been tight, but ever since Lucinda had snuffed out the candle and run out of the secret agent meeting, Kyle had been trying to convince himself that either Lucinda had heard her mom wrong, or her mom hadn't meant what she said.

Far-fetched?

Sure.

But Kyle was desperate. Or, at least, Kyle thought he was desperate until that FOR SALE sign made him want to run as fast as he could and crash into a brick wall. Except it wouldn't have helped. Nothing would. In a month—maybe two—a moving van would be pulling up across the street, and Lucinda would be standing on the sidewalk shaking Kyle's hand good-bye. Or not. Maybe Lucinda would skip the farewell scene altogether since she and Kyle still weren't talking. Not a word.

Not a look. Not since Kyle gave Lucinda the shrug.

Nuts!

That's what I say.

I didn't want to get into this. I was hoping either Kyle or Lucinda would have come to his or her senses by now. But no! Here were two of the smartest, coolest kids you'd ever meet, and it turns out that both of them had a stubborn streak as wide as the Atlantic Ocean.

So okay.

So maybe saying you're sorry can sometimes be a weakness. But only when you *aren't* sorry. And these two were. Only neither would admit it. And worse— way worse—time was running out, and Kyle was totally stumped. Maybe that tourniquet had caused his brain to freeze, or maybe he was so busy being stubborn he couldn't come up with a plan, any plan, to stop Lucinda's mom from running away. Not without talking to Lucinda. And so his brain stayed frozen, and that tourniquet kept twisting the rest of that afternoon and right through supper and all night long until it was Friday morning at 7:05 and Lucinda was sitting on her top step in her wraparound sunglasses waiting for Ruben to pick her up on his way to school. Only this time Kyle didn't just pass by without speaking, as he had for the past six days. This time Kyle opened his door, dropped his backpack on the stoop, and sat on *his* front step. Because he'd had it. Because he was sick of being stubborn. Because he didn't know how much more time he had, and he wanted to set things straight.

Right?

Wrong.

I swear. You should have seen him. Mr. Cool. The Ice Man. Looking up and down the street. Yawning. Stretching. Scratching his arm. Picking up a leaf on the step in front of him. And, no, he didn't crumble it into pieces and toss it aside. He checked it out. He studied it. You heard me. *He studied it! As if Kyle Parker was interested in leaves!*

Lucinda?

The same.

Well, that wasn't exactly true. She wasn't studying leaves. But the rest of it? Oh, yeah! As much as Kyle pretended to ignore her, she pretended to ignore him right back. Which was easy for Lucinda since she was wearing those sunglasses. Which meant Kyle couldn't tell which way she was looking. Though why she cared she had no idea. Since she was leaving town. So the heck with Kyle Parker. Who cared about Kyle Parker? She wouldn't have to worry about Kyle Parker anymore. At least *that* should have made her happy, *right*? Of course it should. You bet it should. So how come she felt like crying all over again?

"Are you waiting for Ruben?" Kyle shouted across the street.

"You know I am," Lucinda shouted back.

And that was when it hit him. Right there in the middle of all those horns honking and people shuffling by on the sidewalk and a garbage truck's air brakes hissing to a halt. That was when Kyle realized what Percy Percerville had meant back at the concrete park yesterday morning. Not the part about Shakespeare wagging his tail. But just after:

"Am I here to help you win the heart of the fair Lucinda? Quite so, dear boy, quite so. Which you would have understood instinctively with a scant perusal of my second novel, *Please, Oh Please,* wherein our deeply troubled protagonist spurns the advances of her darkly handsome love interest until a sinfully beautiful provocateur saunters onto the scene."

27

Did Kyle get an explanation of what any of that was supposed to mean?

Hardly.

No sooner had Percy completed his last sentence than he cocked his eyebrows, swirled his cape in front of his face, and weaved his way down Ninth Avenue. Leaving Kyle . . . Well, you know where it left Kyle. Lost. Dumbfounded. Until this very moment when Kyle finally understood why he was so jealous and Lucinda wasn't. It was exactly as Percy's mumbo jumbo had predicted. It took three. Not two. No one was ever jealous when there were only two. But three. There had to be three. As in Kyle and Lucinda *and* Ruben. Kyle was jealous of *Ruben*. Lucinda was jealous of *nobody*. Because there was *nobody* to be jealous of!

And so Kyle spoke.

He said words. Only the words weren't just words. They were more like a bomb exploding. I'm not saying he raised his voice or that any of the words taken by themselves were all that powerful. But put them all together, and they were dynamite. They were TNT.

"I'm going to meet someone, too," Kyle said.

BOOM!

Lucinda stopped breathing. Pink dots flashed before her eyes. Her body felt as if it had been lifted off the steps and was hovering three feet above the cement. Only it wasn't dreamy. She didn't feel as if she were floating. It was more like vanishing. Like she was drifting away to nothing or that maybe she was never there in the first place.

"Who?"

That was what Lucinda wanted to ask. But she couldn't. Her pride wouldn't let her.

So instead she said, "Congratulations!"

Only when she said it, her lower lip trembled. Just

for an instant. You had to be watching like a hawk to catch it. But Kyle was. He did. Which meant Percy had been right. You needed three. Because sometimes you didn't know how much you liked someone until that person liked someone else. So without thinking, without second-guessing himself, Kyle pushed himself up from that top step, hopped down the stairs, and walked east toward Eighth Avenue.

He didn't glance over his shoulder.

He didn't wave good-bye.

Nothing flashy.

Though you can bet he was pretty darned pleased with himself for finally making a move. A roundabout move, sure, since there certainly wasn't anyone he was about to pick up. But Lucinda didn't know that. As far as she was concerned, Kyle may well have been getting ready to escort the prom queen to her homeroom door. *That* was the point. *That* was why Kyle was so busy patting himself on the back. And it had been easy. No sweat. A single sentence had done it. And, yeah, that sentence may not have been altogether true, but that didn't stop the following chain reaction from ticking off inside Kyle's brain:

You did it.

You made Lucinda jealous.

Which is good.

Great, even.

Though it doesn't really matter.

Not really.

Because Lucinda is still leaving unless you come up with a plan!

THUMP!

Oh, yeah. One thing I haven't mentioned about Kyle yet. He sort of went off in a zone every so often and lost track of his immediate surroundings. Which

29

didn't matter on that seven-and-a-half-minute walk to school since every fire hydrant, curb, and red light had hardwired itself into Kyle's cerebral cortex. Plus, like all New Yorkers, Kyle had a sixth sense when it came to maneuvering past oncoming pedestrians and lunatic taxi drivers. But all that changed the moment Kyle cut through the chain-link fence surrounding Roosevelt High's asphalt courtyard, and his internal radar failed to pick up the brand-new, two-inch, metal handrail installed yesterday afternoon smack dab in the middle of the front steps. Not for long, though. Not after Kyle heard the *THUMP!* thunder in his eardrums and realized it was the outward manifestation of the searing pain shooting up to his brain then ricocheting back down to his kneecap.

"Yow!" Kyle cried.

"Yow?" Tyrone repeated.

That's right. In order to complete Kyle's total humiliation, his fellow secret agent not only happened to arrive at Roosevelt High's front steps just in time to witness Kyle's klutzy move, but also to poke fun at his lamebrain response.

"I didn't see the handrail," Kyle said.

"It's not exactly hidden," Tyrone said.

But here's the thing. Here's why Kyle was Kyle. Yes, he was embarrassed he'd been so spaced-out he hadn't been watching where he was going. And you can bet he wished he'd have come up with a cooler response than "Yow!" But in spite of his knee throbbing and the tops of his ears turning pink, neither was enough to stop an idea from flashing into Kyle's head.

"What are you doing after school?" he said.

"Voice class," Tyrone said.

"Uh-uh," Kyle said. "You just think you are."

CHAPTER 7

Lucinda had a weak spot. More than one, actually, but one in particular made her feel totally insecure at times. Lucinda had no best girlfriend. It wasn't that girls didn't like her. Lucinda was smart, cool, fun, all of that stuff. But girls sort of held Lucinda in awe. Like maybe she was *too* smart or *too* cool or something. Which was *too* bad. Because she sure could have used a best friend now.

For backup.

You heard me—backup.

Best friends are a safety net. Especially when your mom is so scared she's making you leave town, and the guy you've had a crush on practically your whole life tells you he's going to meet someone else then hops down his steps and disappears down Twentieth Street. It was that confidence thing again. And, yeah, as I said before, Lucinda usually had plenty. But that's the thing about confidence. It doesn't always hang around. Sometimes, when we need it most, it tucks its tail between its legs and runs away.

Which, of course, was exactly what happened to Lucinda on that day of all days. Not that you can measure confidence the way you can your heart rate. But on a scale of one to ten, Lucinda's self-esteem was checking in somewhere around minus two. Nor did it pick up when she arrived at school. Though it should have. Since she arrived at school with Ruben.

Let's be honest:

If it's logic we're talking about here, all Lucinda had to do was jot down Kyle's and Ruben's pros and cons, and we all know that the great-looking basketball star would beat the kid with the bony elbows every single time. But who ever said your heart was logical? Certainly not Lucinda. Certainly not after spending the rest of her school day watching Kyle and Tyrone huddle together by the trophy case between classes then eat together in the cafeteria during lunch then cross the asphalt courtyard together after the final bell.

That's right.

Lucinda saw everything. Okay, so she only imagined the cafeteria scene since she didn't have lunch the same period as Kyle and Tyrone. But you can bet Lucinda made sure she saw the rest: the way Tyrone hung on every word, the dead serious look on Kyle's face when he talked and kept talking and never shut up. And, of course, Lucinda convinced herself that she knew exactly what Kyle was saying, that he was telling Tyrone how cool this new girl was, how beautiful, how she wasn't leaving town, how she was staying right here in New York. This was all guesswork on Lucinda's part, of course, since she made sure to keep her distance and stay out of sight until after the final bell when she raced out to the front steps just in time to see Kyle and Tyrone cut through the chain-link fence heading south.

Not west.

Not toward home.

But south.

Toward Greenwich Village with its used CD outlets and way-cool stores and ten zillion other places to hang out. Because that was what kids did. Roosevelt High kids, at least. They met in Greenwich Village after school to hang out. Together. *On dates.* Which, of course, was exactly what Lucinda figured Kyle was up to. He was going to meet that girl again. He was going to introduce her to Tyrone. Why? So they could get to know each other. So Kyle could make sure she fit in. So when the time came and Lucinda left New York, this new girl could become a secret agent and *take Lucinda's place!*

Remember Kyle this morning?

Pathetic Kyle?

Miserable Kyle?

Who thought he'd lost everything forever?

Well, that was Lucinda now as she gripped that same handrail Kyle's left knee had smashed into seven hours before. Only Lucinda wasn't smashing into anything. She was gripping that black, two-inch metal rod as tight as she could. Her teeth clenched. Her eyes at half-mast. No backup. No best girlfriend to tell her everything was going to be okay. Watching Kyle Parker walk out of her life.

CHAPTER 8

Lucinda was right about one thing. Kyle and Tyrone were headed to Greenwich Village. But not to meet the new girl who you and I know didn't even exist. They were headed to Washington Square Park on business.

Secret agent business.

Which meant they didn't sit by the fountain and listen to the guys with the Rasta hair play their steel drums or watch the woman on stilts swallow her sword or juggle her rings of fire. Kyle and Tyrone needed quiet. They needed to concentrate. So they entered the square under that huge arch you always see on all those New York City postcards and stuck to the diagonal crosswalks. They passed street artists and beaded jewelry venders and three guys scalping Knicks playoff tickets. They passed a belly dancing class and a woman in white gloves and a white straw hat walking a cat on a rhinestone leash hooked to a rhinestone collar. And, still, Kyle and Tyrone didn't stop. They kept walking until they found a quiet, shady spot away from the late April sun in the southwest corner of the square on either side of a concrete chess table.

And, no, they didn't play chess.

Don't be silly.

Kyle didn't ask Tyrone to go to Greenwich Village to play chess. The real reason—the reason Kyle had been explaining to Tyrone all day—was that Tyrone had never been to Lucinda's house when her mom was home. Which meant Lucinda's mom didn't know Tyrone. Which meant Lucinda's mom might figure Tyrone was a stranger and let down her guard.

Sure, it was a long shot.

Kyle knew the chance was slim that Lucinda's mom would tell some total stranger—especially a kid—who or what she was hiding from or why she needed proof when she wouldn't even tell her own daughter. But, hey! Lucinda's mom was scared. And maybe she needed a release valve to take off some of the pressure. Maybe she needed to spill her guts to someone safe, someone she didn't know, someone she figured she'd never see again.

Yeah, it sounded crazy. Kyle would have been the first to admit it sounded crazy. But even though it wasn't the greatest plan anyone ever came up with, it was still a plan. And Kyle figured *any* plan—even a plan as farfetched as this one—was better than *no* plan.

"But I have *voice class!*" Tyrone said.

"Cancel!" Kyle said.

"But it's Mozart's *Don Giovanni!*" Tyrone said.

"But this is Lucinda!" Kyle said.

And that was it. That was all Kyle had to say. Because opera may have been the main thing Tyrone thought about day and night, but—unlike Chad—Tyrone realized that once in a while you had to take other people's feelings into consideration. Like your friends, for instance. And Tyrone had always been aware of what Lucinda meant to Kyle, even when Kyle hadn't been aware of it himself. So it didn't matter that Tyrone had never cut a class before (especially *voice* class) and that normally he wouldn't have considered it. This wasn't normally. This was Lucinda and Kyle. So it really wasn't a choice.

As I told you before, in life (real life, everyday life) Tyrone Brown was shy and unsure of himself. He talked to Kyle and the secret agents, sure. But that was about it. Weeks could go by without Tyrone having a conversation with anyone else, especially a girl. Outside of Lucinda, Tyrone rarely spoke to girls. There was no reason for this. Tyrone was tall enough and good-looking enough and smart enough. Plus, he was pretty much the Ruben Gomez of the high school opera world. What I'm saying is, nothing should have held Tyrone back.

And nothing did.

Onstage.

There's this writer named Kurt Vonnegut. He wrote this story called *Who Am I This Time?* It's about this shy guy who totally turns himself into any part he plays in front of an audience: a baseball player, a gorilla, whatever. The guy's an actor, not a singer, but *Who Am I This Time?* was Tyrone's favorite story. Because Tyrone was the guy. If the part he was singing was a pirate, you'd swear he'd grown a hook. If the part he was singing was a murderer, you'd check the shadows when you left the opera house. Okay, so that last one was an overstatement, but you get my meaning.

Kyle certainly did.

He'd seen the transformation more than once. What Kyle hadn't realized, however, was that—as far as Tyrone was concerned—singing was acting, acting was singing,

a part was a part. And, no, Tyrone wouldn't be playing this part on a stage inside a theater. But that didn't matter. Not to Tyrone. As far as Tyrone was concerned, he would be *acting in the theater of life.*

"You want me to lie," Tyrone said.

"I want you to find out why Lucinda's mom wants to leave New York by pretending you're a student," Kyle said. "You know. Like you are right now. Only older."

Abracadabra!

Hocus-pocus!

Tyrone didn't change clothes. He didn't change hair color. He didn't grow a beard. There was nothing obvious about his outward appearance that changed a single, solitary bit. But at the same time, everything changed. A half smile here. A raised eyebrow there. And presto! Tyrone looked like he could have voted in the last two presidential elections.

"I guess you're ready," Kyle said.

"I guess I am," Tyrone said.

And stood up.

And squared his shoulders.

And walked away.

Was there anything about Tyrone's step that said he was the least bit concerned that maybe marching into a college professor's office under false pretenses to try to pry personal information out of her was foolhardy? Uh-uh. I'm not saying Tyrone wasn't nervous. His heart was beating like one of those steel drums. But it was the kind of nerves that performers get just before the curtain goes up. *So what* this wasn't singing. *So what* he was missing his *Don Giovanni* lesson! The square? The street? Even Lucinda's mom's office? They were still a stage. And Tyrone was about to give the performance of his life!

Rationalization?

37

You bet.

But, let's face it, spying is spying. There's no easy way to find out something someone doesn't want you to find out. And it wasn't as if Tyrone's *acting in the theater of life* had anything to do with robbing a bank or cheating on a pop quiz. Or, at least, that was what he kept telling himself with that late April sun now feeling good on his shoulders as he backtracked diagonally across Washington Square then walked the half block east past a Korean fruit stand next to a Vietnamese restaurant next to a Chinese acupuncturist before stopping under what may very well have been the only apricot tree in all of New York City.

"Excuse me. Is this the biology building?"

This was Tyrone, of course. He was addressing his question to a really tall young woman with dark, curly hair sprinkled with chalk dust she hadn't bothered to brush out. The woman had just pushed open a wooden, double door with those metal bars you push to unlatch the lock. Over the door were black block capital letters that spelled out 29 WASHINGTON PLACE, which Kyle had already told Tyrone was the address of NYU's biology department. But the woman was descending the stairs right in front of Tyrone, and she'd just stepped out of the building. Plus, she had the look of someone who certainly might have been a biology student (the chalk dust gave her away), so Tyrone figured he'd ask just to make sure.

"Who are you looking for?" the woman said.

As she said it, she gave Tyrone the once-over. You know—the way women sometimes do when they run across a man of mystery. Because, remember, Tyrone wasn't Tyrone anymore. He was the guy who was playing the guy who was pretending to be a college student.

"I'm looking for Dr. Winston," Tyrone said.

"You mean Professor Winston," the woman said.

"What's the difference?" Tyrone said.

At which point most of us would have mumbled "Nothing" or "Never mind." But, remember, this was a woman with chalk dust in her hair who suddenly found herself talking to a man who made her fingertips tingle and her lips feel numb, so it wasn't all that surprising she might want to keep this conversation going as long as possible, even if it meant passing along some information that really wasn't any of her business to pass along.

"Professor Winston never finished her dissertation," she said.

"So?" Tyrone said.

"So she never got her PhD," the woman said.

Tyrone looked blank.

"Her doctorate in molecular biology back in 1983," the woman said. "Not that she needs it. She knows more about this stuff than anyone on the planet."

"This stuff?"

"Cancer. Cancer cells. Oncology. Are you telling me you don't know her? If not, then maybe I ought to take you down there. Though I've got to warn you. She seems a bit whacked-out today."

Whacked-out?

Today?

Tyrone decided to let this last bit of information slide. No need to push it. He was already way ahead of the game. *Never finished her dissertation? Never got her doctorate in molecular biology?* Who was this woman? The NYU gossip queen? Not that Tyrone was complaining. He hadn't even met Lucinda's mom yet, and he already knew enough to get Kyle's eyes spinning.

"That's okay," Tyrone said. "You don't have to take

me down there. Except I wouldn't mind knowing where *down there* is."

"Two floors. Take the stairs on the left to the dungeon. That's what we call the lab. You'll see why when you get there."

And that was it.

Tyrone was gone.

He scampered up the steps, pushed open the double door, and cut left down the first-floor hallway. And, yeah, he noticed the hundreds of butterflies pinned to the purple velvet inside the glass cases next to the human skeleton next to the plaster of paris replicas of the human digestive, cardiovascular, and reproductive systems. Not that he stopped to admire any of them, especially the human brain floating in formaldehyde in the last case before the stairwell.

Did any of this give him the creeps?

You bet.

Enough so he took the stairs two at a time all the way down to the basement, where one glance told him the chalk dust woman had been right. It looked exactly like a dungeon. No windows. No natural light. Just naked florescent bulbs humming overhead, casting their cold, hard, white-white glare down on the cages upon cages of rats and cats and dogs.

"We don't kill them, if that's what you're worried about."

Tyrone had seen *The Grudge* and *The Ring* and even *The Ring Two*. He'd had bums on the sidewalk pull on his shirtsleeve and beg for quarters. He'd broken his left ankle. He'd had braces put on and taken off his teeth. He'd been sideswiped by a motorcycle. He'd had his appendix taken out. But none of that stuff had prepared him for the jolt he got from the eyes of the woman wearing the lab coat.

40

Whacked-out?

I guess!

The woman had to be Lucinda's mom. No one else was around. And it wasn't as if Professor Winston was foaming at the mouth or snarling. But her eyes! They were empty. No, not empty. Missing. As if they weren't there at all. I mean, Professor Winston was. She was standing right next to an electron microscope. But her eyes weren't. They were gone. Out of there. Like they'd already moved to Atlanta.

"Kill them?" Tyrone said.

"The animals," Professor Winston said. "After we're finished with the experiments."

"I'm not worried."

"Of course you are. Everyone is. Me too. Which is why we don't. Some labs do. But this is my lab and my rules."

"Oh."

"Oh is right. And you are?"

"Edward Brown."

He couldn't use his real name, of course. Lucinda's mom may never have met Tyrone, but she certainly knew the names of the secret agents. So Kyle suggested Tyrone use a name as close to his real name as possible. Which was exactly what Tyrone did. He chose his middle and last name. And thank goodness! Because Tyrone was already plenty mixed up as it was and figured he was doing awfully well just to remember his *middle* name.

"You're my new assistant?" Professor Winston said.

"No," Tyrone said. "No, I'm not. I'm just looking at the school. I'm thinking of applying."

Which was true.

Sort of.

Tyrone *was* thinking of applying to school. Just not to

NYU. Though that didn't mean he couldn't start. Now, for instance. And, no, he wouldn't be applying for a while, and he certainly wouldn't be applying in the field of biology, even though he was standing in the biology department speaking to a member of the biology staff, so it wasn't too surprising Lucinda's mom figured he was. What *was* surprising, however, was Professor Winston's response.

"Are you sure?" she said.

Innocent enough, right?

Her hands didn't shoot over her mouth. Her eyes didn't bulge out of their sockets. But, then, you didn't hear the *way* Professor Winston said what she just said. It was like a warning. Like Professor Winston just shouted: "No! Don't even think about applying! Not here! Leave this instant! Run home! Lock your door! Move to Italy! Never set foot in this building again!"

A half an hour ago, if you had asked Tyrone what the odds were of this spy scheme actually working, he'd have said one in ten, tops. People didn't pour their guts out to strangers except maybe in the movies or on TV and only then because it was in the script. Not for real. Never for real. Except here he was. No fuss. No muss. First the woman with the chalk dust blabbing like crazy, and now Lucinda's mom ready to tell everything, and all Tyrone had to do was ask one simple question:

"What do you mean, 'Are you sure?'"

That was it. That was all Tyrone had to ask. In fact, he was about to ask it. Only he was waiting that extra beat. He was letting the pressure build. Not inside himself. He was letting it build inside Lucinda's mom. Like a volcano about to blow. Had to blow. Tyrone could tell all he had to do was give it one more nudge.

"What—," Tyrone started to say.

But he stopped.

He was cut off. Not by Lucinda's mom. Tyrone was cut off by someone's feet shuffling behind him. And so he spun. He froze—bug-eyed—staring straight at Lucinda. Who—bug-eyed—was staring straight back.

CHAPTER 9

Lucinda couldn't blink. She couldn't unlock her eyelids. She had to concentrate with all her might to stop herself from crumbling to the floor. Seeing that lost, faraway look in her mom's eyes was bad enough. But seeing it in front of someone she knew was worse. Way worse. She had no idea what Tyrone would say or who he'd say it to. Kyle, for instance. Would Tyrone tell Kyle? What was Tyrone doing in the NYU biology lab anyway? Did he come on his own, or did somebody send him? Was it Kyle? Did *he* send Tyrone?

Of course!

Had to be!

Lucinda saw it as clear as anything she'd ever seen in her life. It *was* Kyle who'd sent Tyrone. Because of the secret agent meeting! Because Lucinda said *her mom* was forcing her family to move to Atlanta! And, yeah, it took him long enough, but Kyle must have finally come up with a plan. That was why he huddled with Tyrone by the trophy case between classes and walked with him to Greenwich Village. So Kyle could coach Tyrone. So Tyrone could get Lucinda's mom to talk. Tyrone was

trying to get Lucinda's mom to say why she wanted to leave New York because she didn't know Tyrone, so maybe—just maybe—she might say something she wouldn't normally say to someone she knew.

Not bad, huh?

Lucinda was quick. So quick she even knew that Kyle had guessed right. Her mom would have talked. She wanted to talk. Lucinda could tell the moment she walked into the lab and saw the steel curtain in front of her mom's eyes had lifted. But that was just it. Lucinda walked in. And the steel curtain slammed back down and would stay down. Not that Lucinda's mom knew Tyrone had come to spy on her. But her mom knew this much. She knew Tyrone knew Lucinda. Which meant Tyrone was no longer a stranger. Which meant the secret agent fact-finding expedition was a bust. Though that didn't mean Lucinda was about to trash the whole operation.

Uh-uh.

No way.

Because Kyle was on the case. Kyle was trying to keep Lucinda in New York. He had to be, or Tyrone wouldn't have been standing in Lucinda's mom's lab. Wait a minute! Wait a minute! Did that mean Kyle liked Lucinda? Even though he wouldn't admit it? Even though he pretended to like another girl?

It didn't matter.

Not at that exact moment.

Since all that mattered was Tyrone was here and Lucinda had blown it, so Lucinda had to salvage whatever she could without wasting her precious energy thinking about Kyle Parker.

"Tyrone!" Lucinda said.

"Lucinda!" Tyrone said.

"I thought you said your name was Edward," Lucinda's mom said.

45

"That's my middle name," Tyrone said. "I was thinking of changing it when I went to college."

"Changing it?" Lucinda's mom said.

"You know," Tyrone said. "Like a brand-new start."

Okay. Not bad. That sounded plausible enough. Tyrone's voice didn't shake. He didn't drop his eyes. And Lucinda? The same. No one could have guessed her whole future in New York City was on the line here.

"This is my mother," Lucinda said.

"Really!" Tyrone said.

"Really," Lucinda said. "Mom, this is Tyrone. Tyrone, this is my mom, Professor Winston."

"Nice to meet you, Professor Winston," Tyrone said.

"Nice to meet *you*, Tyrone. Or should I say Edward?" Professor Winston said.

She said it like she bought it, like she didn't suspect a thing. Which was good. Of course it was good. But Lucinda knew she couldn't just leave it there. She had to keep the conversation moving. She couldn't give her mom a whole lot of time to think, or she might come to the conclusion that one of her daughter's friends showing up in the NYU biology lab at this particular moment was a bit more than a coincidence.

"Are you looking into NYU's voice program?" Lucinda said.

"Voice program?" Lucinda's mom said.

"Sure, Mom," Lucinda said. "Tyrone's the best high school opera singer in New York City."

"Really?" Lucinda's mom said. "I just figured since he was standing in NYU's biology lab talking to an NYU biology professor that he might be interested in the Bachelor of Science program in biology. How silly of me. My mistake. By all means, Tyrone, apply to NYU. It's one of the greatest universities in the world. You can pick up information online or at the admissions office.

And if you're still interested, send me your transcripts and letters of recommendation. I'll be leaving the department at the end of this semester, but I'll certainly do anything I can to help a friend of Lucinda's."

"Thank you," Tyrone said.

"You're welcome," Professor Winston said.

Weird.

Crazy.

That steel curtain was gone again.

Lucinda's mom was back looking like Lucinda's mom. In charge. A professional at the top of her game. Which reminded Lucinda of the reason she'd come to her mom's lab in the first place. Lucinda had come to apologize for yelling yesterday morning and sulking around the house ever since.

Though that was only part of the reason.

The real reason was to announce that boys—all boys but especially Kyle Parker—were about as fickle as you could get and that it was just fine with her to leave New York as quick as they could and move to Atlanta. But then Tyrone was here. And Lucinda suddenly realized Kyle wasn't fickle after all. And even if he were, it still wouldn't matter since Lucinda also realized that if she left New York now without putting up a fight she'd be doing what her mom was doing. Lucinda would be hiding. And twenty years from now it might be her own daughter staring at Lucinda, wondering why her mom was always running away.

"He's not just my friend," Lucinda said. "He's also a secret agent."

"Of course he is, dear," Lucinda's mom said. "All your friends are secret agents."

"Just like all my friends are smart enough to know that you don't come to a biology lab to apply to college," Lucinda said. "Not if you're a voice major. Tyrone

47

is here because Kyle sent him. Because Kyle is trying to find out what I'm trying to find out. He's trying to find out why we're moving. Oh, come on, Mom! Stop it! Don't look at me like that! Tell me what you were about to tell someone you didn't even know!"

Silence.

Total.

The rats in their cages quit riding the wheel. The cats quit hissing. The dogs quit howling. Maybe they sensed the tension. Or maybe they heard Lucinda's heart ticking like a time bomb. Was this it? Was this the breakthrough? Would her mom finally crack?

"I *can't*!" Professor Winston said, her voice practically a whisper. "Lucinda! Sweetheart! I know you're a secret agent! I know you think you can help! But it's exactly like I told your father! I have no proof! He will ruin me! He will ruin our family!"

CHAPTER 10

"Who?"

That was what Lucinda wanted to scream. It was what she almost screamed. But she didn't. She knew it wouldn't do any good. She knew her mother would just clam up. So Lucinda stopped herself just in the nick of time by clamping her teeth down on the insides of her lips, and out of the corner of her eyes she saw Tyrone was doing the same thing.

Which meant Lucinda was right.

Her mom had just slipped.

Right there in the basement of the NYU biology building in her very own laboratory, Lucinda's mom had given them a clue and said it was a *he* she was afraid of. And that was before Tyrone could get Lucinda off by herself and give her the lowdown on her mom's unfinished dissertation and how NYU had hired her anyway. Which would make three. Three clues. Just like that. Toss in Lucinda's logic and creativity, and who knows where the three clues might lead?

Not us, I'm afraid.

Or, at least, not yet.

Because we can't stay. Because something even more extraordinary was about to happen. To Chad. Fifty blocks north at Serendipity. That's right. *The* Serendipity on Sixtieth Street. The place in the movie where John Cusack and Kate Beckinsale fall in love over a frozen hot chocolate.

But for real.

Serendipity, I mean.

It's real. People eat there. Famous people. Melanie Griffith and Jodie Foster and Bruce Willis, for instance. They eat there with their kids. Who are famous by association. Which was one of the reasons Chad traveled forty blocks north to eat at Serendipity at least once a week. Sure, he loved the frozen hot chocolate. *Everyone* does. But Chad was also hoping that maybe, just maybe, if he ate at Serendipity he might become famous, too. *By association.*

Backward logic?

You bet.

But, remember, this was Chad. The same guy who, three years before, had tried to become Spider-Man by almost letting a black widow bite him on the arm. (He didn't. He either came to his senses in the nick of time, or he chickened out. I'll let you decide which.)

For the record, Chad would probably have come to Serendipity even if no one famous had ever stepped foot inside the place. And you would too, every chance you got, since it's pretty much the equivalent of devouring a hot fudge sundae while riding the Space Mountain roller coaster at Disney World. Not the loop-de-loop part. But the noise. The action. The line out the door with kids jammed into the gift shop or squirming their way along the white tile floor under the ten zillion halogen lights *and* Tiffany lamps. Yeah, it's bright. Way bright. Bright enough for everyone to see the gigantic grandfather clock with its arms that keep spinning but never tell the right time.

It was the reason Chad sat there.

At the table under the clock, I mean.

He sat there because the kids who passed always stared at the spinning arms, so Chad liked to pretend they were staring at him. Only today was different. Today there was this old guy sitting in the very same chair where Chad always sat. The guy was sixty at least with this pencil-thin mustache and his hair parted down the middle. He was sitting at the table by himself, but he didn't *seem* to be sitting by himself. He was the kind of guy who caught your attention because he wasn't paying attention to anyone else. Why bother? As far as he was concerned, he was the most important person in the room. Which floored Chad. Totally. Since Chad *always* paid attention to *everyone* else.

What did it mean?

The guy had to be big! A movie star! A game show host! A guy who did infomercials on cable TV! Who? Who was this guy? Chad couldn't place him. But that didn't stop Chad from staring. In fact, Chad stared so long he forgot to look where he was going. Which, at the moment, was straight into a two-year-old in a high chair with whipped cream all over his face.

"Ow!"

Fortunately, that wasn't the two-year-old screaming. It was Chad, whose red and gray Adidas bumped the back left leg of the two-year-old's high chair, and then Chad screamed as only Chad could scream, stopping the clanging and clattering and chattering as every waitress, waiter, grandma, grandpa, mom, dad, aunt, uncle, and kid swung his or her head around toward the huge boy wearing the WHO'S OBNOXIOUS? T-shirt grabbing for his big toe, missing it, and stumbling forward out of control.

"Watch it!"

Smash!

"Whoa!"

Crash!

"Ow!"

Chad careened off chairs, banged into the back of a woman wearing a polka-dot dress, spun, tripped over his own two feet, then flew—belly first—hitting the marble-topped table under the grandfather clock. He hit it in a sort of a swan dive as his flinging left arm caught the old guy's frozen hot chocolate and sent it flying *splat* into the old guy's herringbone sports coat. We're talking a lake. A flood. As if the old guy's breast pocket had just been hit by a gigantic mud balloon.

Silence!

Dead silence!

Followed by gasps. Then giggles. Until everyone all around exploded in laughter. Think of a volcano erupting or an avalanche roaring down a mountain. That was what it sounded like to Chad. But you know something? The disgrace and humiliation wasn't the worst of it. Uh-uh. It was the other thing. The thing no one else in Serendipity saw. Not the birthday party at the next table. Not the manager and waiter running over to help.

Chad saw the look.

The old guy's look.

Because, remember, Chad wasn't alone in this. Everyone in Serendipity was laughing at the old guy too. Who wasn't used to being laughed at. You could tell by his eyes, which were filled with such red-hot hate that if he could he would have breathed fire and burned Chad alive. And that wasn't the end of it. There was also the chill. From the old guy's heart? From his soul? Chad wasn't sure. But he was sure he felt it. Fire and ice in the same look. And then it was gone. In a flash. An instant. But that instant was enough. It was like sticking your finger into a wall socket. Chad felt the jolt shoot right up his spine.

I know.

I know.

We're talking about a sixty-year-old guy in a herringbone sports coat here. No way was Chad going to admit he was scared of some sixty-year-old guy with a pencil-thin mustache.

"It's all your fault!" Chad cried. "I never would have slipped if you hadn't been sitting in my seat!"

The fire and ice may have been gone, but it was replaced by a look so arrogant most people may have been tempted to toss another frozen hot chocolate in the old guy's face.

But not Chad.

Not even close.

All Chad saw or heard or cared about was the old guy's raised chin and cocked eyebrows as he snapped his finger at the manager then pointed at Chad then pointed at the door.

And that was it.

The old guy never said a word.

It was as if he were giving commands to a not-so-bright housepet. "Fetch! Roll over! Get my slippers! Lick my feet!" That was the old guy's attitude. And, sure, the manager could have said, "Excuse me, sir. Human beings don't snap their finger at one another," but it *was* Chad who'd spilled the frozen hot chocolate, ruined the sports coat, and put a dent in the old guy's overblown pride.

"Eli?" the manager said.

The waiter gently but firmly locked his right hand around Chad's left elbow, and before Chad knew what was what he found himself shuffling his feet on the

Sixtieth Street sidewalk with only a vague recollection of being escorted outside.

"Don't worry, sport," Eli said.

"Sport?" Chad said.

"You bet," Eli said. "What better name for the guy who ruined the old man's coat? Hey, I'm not complaining. I only met him half an hour ago when he pushed his way through the door, brushed past twenty people standing in line, and parked himself at our most popular table. 'My name is Harry Templeton,' he told me as if I was already supposed to know. 'Doesn't ring a bell? Pity. Though it says more about your education than it does about my name.' He took the menu I handed him and tossed it aside. 'Listen closely,' he said, 'because I never repeat myself. Every day, for as many days as I see fit, I shall be eating lunch at this very table. Tomorrow, for instance. Saturday. I will be here at eleven thirty sharp. Understood? Grand! Now it's off to the kitchen with you double-time, and don't even think about returning without a frozen hot chocolate and a Maraschino cherry on top.'"

Gee!

Don't you wish he was *your* grandpa?

Me, neither.

But Chad wasn't hearing Eli give a point-by-point rundown of what a jerk Harry Templeton was so Chad wouldn't feel bad about the herringbone coat. Chad heard the exact opposite. In fact, the more Eli talked, the more Chad tried to convince himself that one day—if he worked on it hard enough—he might even become as arrogant and self-centered as the great Harry Templeton.

Extraordinary?

You bet.

But things were about to become even more extra-

ordinary. You see, Chad hadn't come to Serendipity to spy on Harry Templeton. Chad didn't care that Harry Templeton had just arrived at LaGuardia Airport that very morning and hadn't lived in New York City since 1983. Chad didn't even know that 1983 was the same year Lucinda's mom never finished her dissertation. Nor did Chad care. Chad had come to Serendipity to eat a frozen hot chocolate and pretend to be famous by association. But that's the thing about going undercover. Sometimes you pick up clues that lead to more clues. And sometimes when you're not even looking for clues—when you couldn't care less about clues—you stumble across the biggest clue of your life.

"Is he famous?" Chad said.

"Seems so," Eli said. "When I came back from the kitchen with his frozen hot chocolate, instead of drinking it he scooped out the cherry and dangled it in front of my face. 'Reminds me of my party tomorrow night at the Museum of Natural History,' he said. '*My* party. In *my* honor. Call it the cherry to top off my career. I've just returned from twenty-three years at UCLA to become head of the biology department at NYU.'"

You get it, right?

NYU?

The biology department?

Harry Templeton was about to become Lucinda's mom's new boss. Or he would have become her boss if Lucinda's mom had been planning to stay at her job. But she wasn't. She was skipping town the same time Harry Templeton was taking over her department.

Serendipity?

You bet.

Not the place.

The word.

It means fate. Good fate. A fortunate discovery by accident. But come on! This went way beyond accident. What were the chances of Chad splattering Lucinda's mom's new biology boss with frozen hot chocolate? A zillion to one? Ten zillion? Wait a minute. Wait a minute. I've got an even better one. What were the chances of it happening at a place called Serendipity?

No way.

Impossible.

Except it happened.

And, almost as impossible, Chad got it. He realized he'd stumbled onto something big, something that would make the other secret agents flip. And since Chad spent most of his waking hours trying to get *anyone* to flip over *anything*, Chad wasn't about to waste any more precious time. He lumbered off that sidewalk like a charging rhinoceros. No "Good-bye, Eli." No "Excuse me" to the woman Chad nearly knocked into the oncoming traffic as he lurched into the street.

His cell phone?

Please!

This information had to be delivered in person. To Kyle. To the secret agents. Because Chad had to see Kyle's face. Chad had to see all of their faces. Too bad Twentieth Street was forty blocks away.

Too bad for Kyle.

Who could have used some news. Any news. The sooner the better. Because at that very moment—the moment Chad was making his mad dash away from Serendipity—Kyle was sitting in his living room banging his fists on the arms of a cracked leather chair. Kyle was jumpy. Which was putting it mildly. Because it was now five o'clock. Five p.m. Seventeen hundred hours. And it didn't matter if Kyle repeated it the long way, the short way, or the military way, it had still been an hour and forty-five minutes since he'd watched Tyrone disappear behind the fountain in Washington Square.

And that was the last Kyle had heard or seen of Tyrone. Tyrone hadn't called. He hadn't knocked on Kyle's door. Was Lucinda's mom giving Tyrone a personal tour of the campus? Was she granting him early enrollment? How long did it take to pretend you were a future biology student to get the goods on someone?

Three minutes? Five minutes? *In and out.* That had been Kyle's orders. Quick and clean. No mentioning that you're really an opera singer. No flourishes. No personal stuff. The longer you stayed, the more chance of a slipup.

Was that it?

Had Tyrone blown his cover? Had Lucinda's mom discovered Tyrone was really a spy and called the cops? How many years could you get for impersonating a future college student?

Okay.

Okay.

This last little bit was even too much for Kyle. Sure, he was nervous. Sure, it was horrible just sitting in his living room waiting. But he'd already walked Shakespeare and eaten a banana and read the *NYU Gazette* on the Internet and discovered that the NYU basketball team stunk and the rowing team stunk even worse and that John T. Beecham (the head of the biology department) was recuperating from a hip operation at some hospital on Roosevelt Island. But there was nothing about Lucinda's mom. No facts. No gossip. No leads to follow. Nothing for Kyle to do but bang on the arms of that cracked leather chair while he waited. And waited. And waited.

Buzz!

The doorbell!

Finally!

But Kyle didn't leap out of the chair and race across the room. Tyrone had taken his time, so Kyle would take his. No big deal. No one's future was on the line. Or so Kyle tried telling himself until he swung open the door and saw it wasn't Tyrone at all but Ruben standing on the front stoop.

"Lucinda doesn't like me," Ruben said.

"Huh?" Kyle said.

"She likes me okay. She just doesn't like me enough."

"Why are you telling me this?"

"Because she ignored me all day. Because she spent the whole day staring at you."

Kyle was so stunned you could have knocked him over. Or, at least, Ruben could have. All he had to do was push. One finger would have done it, and Kyle would have been flat on his back. I mean, here Kyle had been worried sick over Tyrone. Where was Tyrone? What was going on with Tyrone? And now Ruben arrived out of the blue and told Kyle this? What did it mean? What was Kyle supposed to make of it? Was Ruben telling Kyle that Lucinda liked *him*?

No!

Couldn't be!

Could it?

Kyle didn't know. Kyle didn't know much of anything at that moment other than Ruben was no longer on Kyle's front doorstep. Not that Ruben marched off in a huff. Far from it. Ruben had taken Kyle's stunned silence as an invitation and simply slipped past Kyle into the living room and was now sitting on the wicker rocker waiting for Kyle to close the front door. It wasn't a conscious thing. Neither one thought about it. It was more like an unspoken truce.

"Back to business," Ruben said.

"Business?" Kyle said.

"Secret agent business. Whatever is going on between you and me and Lucinda, I still want her to stay in New York."

"Me, too. So?"

"So Tyrone called me."

"Tyrone called *you*?"

"He's with Lucinda," Ruben said. "Something's up.

Something about her mom's dissertation twenty-three years ago back in 1983. She never finished it. That's why Tyrone called. He wanted me to get you and meet them at the library, so we can all try to find out why."

Buzz!

CHAPTER 12

"Chad?" Kyle said.

He said this right after he swung open his front door for the second time in the last three minutes. Though Chad didn't answer. Not right away. Not before he stepped inside. Sorry, did I say *stepped*? It was more like *leaped*. Chad didn't answer before he *leaped* inside. And Kyle and Ruben weren't sure. The light inside Kyle's living room wasn't all that hot. But they could have sworn their fellow secret agent was so excited there were bubbles foaming out of the side of his mouth.

"Harry Templeton!" Chad shouted.

"What?" Kyle said.

"I just knocked a frozen hot chocolate all over Harry Templeton's sports coat at Serendipity!" Chad said.

"Congratulations," Ruben said.

"You're not hearing me!" Chad said. "Harry Templeton! The coolest guy ever! I just met him today! I splattered his sports coat with frozen hot chocolate! See! I have it all over me, too! We both have it all over ourselves! And he likes the same table I like! He likes it so much he's going back tomorrow at eleven thirty and sitting at that very same table. Get it? Get what I'm saying?"

"You and Harry Templeton like the same table at Serendipity," Kyle said.

"That's right!" Chad said. "But that's not the best part! The best part is he's going to be Lucinda's mom's new boss! Can you believe it? Can you believe how lucky she is? All we have to do is tell her, and she'll change her mind! No way is she ever going to want to leave New York! Not now! Not when she finds out about his party tomorrow night at the Museum of Natural History. Because he's back! He's been gone from NYU for twenty-three years, but now he's back!"

"What did you just say?" Kyle said.

"Did you say twenty-three years?" Ruben said.

"Yeah!" Chad said. "Twenty-three years! That's exactly what I—"

But neither Kyle nor Ruben stuck around for the end of that sentence. They were gone. Like a shot. Chad couldn't believe it. All Kyle and Ruben seemed to care about was one fact and one fact only: *Harry Templeton had been gone from NYU for twenty-three years, and now he was back!* The two of them flew up Kyle's stairs and into his room and hunched over his computer and Googled "Harry Templeton" before Chad even got the chance to mention how Harry Templeton had snapped his fingers at the manager. Why? Because Kyle and Ruben didn't need a library. Unlike Lucinda and Tyrone, Kyle and Ruben had a name. And three seconds later they had 2,567 hits flashing across the screen. And every single one of them referred to an article Harry Templeton had published in the *New England Journal of Medicine* in December, 1983, called *The Receptor-Lock Key.*

Just like that!

Kyle and Ruben found it!

All the sites agreed!

The Receptor-Lock Key was the article. The discovery. The medical breakthrough that had changed Harry Templeton's life. More than that, it had changed science. Because this wasn't just any old article we're talking about here. All that mumbo-jumbo about cells and molecules and chains of proteins was so brilliant and revolutionary it might someday stop the big C! Cancer! Harry Templeton had come up with a theory so astounding that medical research would be working on it for the next fifty years!

"And it was written in 1983!" Kyle said.

"The same year Lucinda's mom *didn't* finish her dissertation!" Ruben said.

"Meaning what?" Chad said.

He'd followed them up the stairs and into Kyle's bedroom, but once again Chad didn't get an answer to his question. Kyle was too busy printing the article, sticking the eight and a half pages inside his pants pocket, and racing back down the stairs with Ruben right behind him. They busted out the front door, waved at a passing cab, hopped inside, and shouted, "The Public Library at Forty-second Street!" at the exact same moment Chad's butt plopped down on the backseat beside them.

"Meaning what?" Chad repeated. "Ruben just said *the same year Lucinda's mom didn't finish her dissertation.* What's that supposed to mean?"

"We'll see," Kyle said.

"We'll see what?" Chad said.

"Lucinda will know," Ruben said.

"Lucinda will know what?" Chad said.

And so it went.

On and on.

Chad was relentless. He never shut up. All through the stop-and-go traffic across town, Chad kept asking the same questions, and Kyle and Ruben kept giving Chad the same brush-off until the cab finally skidded to a stop at Forty-second Street. Which was when Kyle and Ruben handed the cabby three bucks each, and Chad dumped eight quarters and ten dimes into the cabby's hand, and then the three of them hopped out of the back door and went racing past Patience and Fortitude, those concrete kings of the jungle guarding the library steps.

"Wait a minute! Wait a minute!" Chad shouted, gasping halfway up the stairs. "I get it! I get it now! You think he stole it, don't you? That's why you printed the article and brought it with you! You think Harry Templeton stole Lucinda's mom's dissertation! You think he stole it and used it for his breakthrough! You think it's his fault Lucinda has to leave town! But it isn't! He didn't! He wouldn't have! Not Harry Templeton! You don't know him like I do!"

Kyle didn't answer.

Neither did Ruben.

Not only because they were sick of answering but also because they had to keep their voices down since they'd just pushed through the rotating doors and were crossing the marble floor of the library's grand entrance hall on their way to the microfilm room with its low ceiling and metal filing cabinets and rows and rows of projectors. Which was where they found Lucinda and Tyrone. They were all by themselves in the very last row hunched over their projectors, staring at their screens, and spinning their 1983 newspaper film: day after day, week after week, month after month. Lucinda had the *New York Times*. Tyrone had the *Post*. Both had made it to April. Neither had found a thing.

"It took you long enough," Tyrone said.

Only Kyle barely heard it. He was too busy staring

at Lucinda, who was busy staring at him—*really* staring at him—for the first time in a long time. And the smile in her eyes nearly made Kyle forget the eight and a half pages in his back jeans pocket.

"You have to read this," he said.

"Read what?" Lucinda said.

"Something by a guy I know," Chad said.

"A guy you know?" Lucinda said.

"Yeah!" Chad said. "A great guy! A cool guy! The best!"

"And why would I want to read an essay by a guy Chad knows?" Lucinda said. "Even if he *is* the best?"

"Because he's being honored tomorrow night for coming back to NYU after twenty-three years," Kyle said.

And that was all Lucinda needed to hear. She grabbed those eight and a half pages out of Kyle's hand and read them straight through. And the way she nodded every few sentences made it clear she understood every single word right down to the very end when she tossed the article on the floor and rolled her eyes back up. Only her attention was no longer focused on Kyle. Nope. Her eyes were shooting daggers straight into the shrinking pupils of you-know-who.

"*This* is who you call a great guy?" she said.

"That's right," Chad said.

Or he would have said it if Lucinda hadn't already sprung out of her chair and lunged at his throat.

CHAPTER 13

"It's stolen!" Lucinda screamed. "All of it! My mom wrote this! Your *great* guy is a *thief!*"

Lucinda didn't get every one of those words out while making her lunge. Everything following "It's" pretty much got muffled by Kyle's shoulder after he did a bit of lunging on his own. Because Kyle had anticipated her reaction. Which was fortunate. Since the clock was ticking, and the secret agents didn't have time for a fight, especially a fight Chad was sure to lose and then never shut up about.

"Are you sure?" Kyle said.

"Am I sure?" Lucinda repeated.

"Yeah," Kyle said. "Are you sure Harry Templeton stole it?"

"When my mom was a kid," Lucinda said, "she never collected dolls or rode horses or tried out for the cheerleading squad. She was too busy winning science fairs. When she was eight, she proved that inside a vacuum a feather and ball bearing are pulled by gravity at the same speed. When she was fifteen, she designed a convertible that wouldn't mess up your hair at seventy miles per hour.

Then her favorite Aunt Harriet got cancer. After that, my mom forgot about vacuums and wind tunnels, and it was all microscopes and petri dishes all the time."

Lucinda stopped.

She took a deep breath.

"The Receptor-Lock Key," she said. "It comes down to one concept: Cells split. Good cells split. Bad cells split. It's how we grow. The trouble is, when the bad cells split, we get sick. So we want to stop it. That's where *The Receptor-Lock Key* comes in. If you slip a chain of proteins inside the receptor where the cell splits and break that chain of proteins (like a key breaking inside a lock), then that cell can't split (like a door can't open). Nothing can get in. Nothing can get out. That's the theory. That's what's so amazing. We're talking about a potential cure here. A long way off maybe. But a way to someday actually stop the spread of cancer."

Again, Lucinda stopped.

Again, she took a deep breath.

"I grew up on this theory," she said. "My dad has explained it to me maybe a million times. Not my mom. My dad. Even though it's not his field. Even though my mom has always left the room. I always figured it was because my mom spent her whole day working on the stuff and didn't want to talk about it when she got home. But today I find out my mom never finished her dissertation, and now you show me an article with the very same words I've been hearing all my life."

Silence.

The secret agents all shut up. They stopped breathing. They stopped swallowing. Everything about them went still except for their eyes, which began darting back and forth around the room as if they were looking for a hidden camera. Because it just occurred to every one of them (Chad included) that a law had been broken.

Harry Templeton had stolen Lucinda's mother's *idea* and, with it, her *career*. Because that was the other thing Kyle and Ruben had discovered on the Internet. Harry Templeton was a star. He'd been interviewed by every major magazine in the country. He'd presented lectures in every major capital in the world. He'd received honorary doctorates from Harvard, Princeton, and Duke.

He was the *man*.

The *authority*.

The *go-to guy*.

Did anyone bother to ask why he hadn't had a major breakthrough in over twenty years?

Uh-uh.

No way.

Harry Templeton had come up with the idea. He'd thought out of the box and written the article that started it all. Cancer could be stopped. Harry Templeton had shown the world how to stop it. And now, if you don't mind, he'd just as soon leave it to the little guys to fill in the details.

Which meant the stakes had suddenly changed. The secret agents were no longer just trying to help Lucinda's mom. They were also trying to destroy a world-renowned scientist's career. And their shoulders—along with the hair on the back of their necks—started to remind them that a guy who'd been living a lie for twenty-three years might be able to come up with one or two not-so-pleasant ways of preventing a few punk kids from exposing that lie.

"So how come your mother never busted him?" Ruben said.

"I don't have a clue," Lucinda said.

"Because she couldn't," Kyle said. "Because Harry Templeton would have made it impossible. Think about it. He must have swiped everything—her notes, her computer files—everything she worked on. Sounds crazy. But she was the student, and he was the teacher. He was in charge. And smart, too. Like a fox. He figured out right away that Lucinda's mom was onto something so big it would not only change her career but also change science. So Harry Templeton warned her: *Tell no one. Trust no one. Not a soul.* And she bought it. She saved her work in only one place on one computer, and the only guy she trusted was the one guy she *never* should have trusted. Because the moment she finally made the big breakthrough, Harry Templeton swiped what she'd written, destroyed every stick of evidence, and warned her not to blab or he'd call her a liar. And who do you suppose the people would believe? Some lowly graduate student or some big-deal college professor who'd been working on this stuff for years?"

"How do you know all that?" Chad said.

"He doesn't," Ruben said. "He's guessing. But it *could* be true."

"Except somebody else knew," Kyle said. "Somebody else besides Lucinda's mom and Harry Templeton. Because no one would have hired her to teach at NYU without finishing her dissertation unless . . ."

"Unless what?" Chad said.

"Unless whoever hired her knew why she didn't finish it," Lucinda said.

And that was it.

That was all Kyle needed to hear.

He turned on his heel, shot past those rows of metal filing cabinets, and bolted for the door. And, yeah, the florescent lights were flickering on and off, which meant it was ten minutes before the library closed at six, but that wasn't why Kyle split. It was because he just remembered something he'd read in the *NYU Gazette* online two hours before that he hadn't thought was important at the time but now seemed as important as the air he was breathing as he beat it down that wide-open hallway:

John T. Beecham, the grand old man of NYU biology, who has been head of the department for the past thirty-five years, is recovering from a hip operation at the Glenmore Memorial Hospital on Roosevelt Island.

John T. Beecham had been the head of the biology department for thirty-five years! That meant he'd been the head in 1983! That meant he would have been the one who hired Lucinda's mom! That meant John T. Beecham must have known about *The Receptor-Lock Key*! He must have! Or he never would have hired her! And John T. Beecham was recovering in Glenmore Memorial Hospital on Roosevelt Island across the East River only four subway stops away on the F train!

But what if Kyle was wrong?

What if John T. Beecham hired Lucinda's mom for some other reason and had no idea what Kyle was talking about? And even if John T. Beecham knew exactly what Kyle was talking about, it wasn't as if the whole secret agent gang could just jam into a hospital room where someone was recovering from major surgery and demand an explanation. That was why Kyle took off from the others. That was why he made his getaway without telling them where he was going. This had to be handled delicately. Quietly. Kyle couldn't be responsible for making a sick man worse, even if Kyle was trying to keep Lucinda from leaving New York and stopping any more harm from happening to her mom. So he didn't say good-bye to the secret agents. He didn't tell them where he was going. He zipped past those metal filing cabinets, shot through that empty hallway, and pushed himself out through the revolving front door.

And still he didn't stop.

He cut left on the diagonal down the concrete steps, hid behind Fortitude so his fellow secret agents couldn't see him even if they chased after him, took a deep breath, flipped open his cell phone, and punched the speed dial button. Because it was now eight minutes to six. The sun would be going down in the next fifty-five minutes, and Kyle Parker may have been a secret agent, but he was also the son of Polly Parker, and he was supposed to be home for dinner at six o'clock.

"Mom?"

"Kyle? Aren't you supposed to be walking through the front door right about now? Not that it's any of my business. I just happen to be your mother."

Okay.

So I haven't given you too many details about Kyle's mom. Kyle's dad—the famous author—was out in L.A. working on the screenplay for *Love in Autumn*. We already know that. Kyle's mom, however, was a different story. Kyle's mom was right there in Manhattan and had to be dealt with. By Kyle. Especially since it was eight minutes to six. And Kyle could tell—even over his cell phone—that his mom was talking to him in that tone every kid recognizes when it's time for supper and he'd better have a very good explanation why he isn't standing two feet in front of her with his hands washed, ready to set the table.

"Mom?"

"Kyle?"

Maybe it was the way his mom said *Kyle?* the second time around as if she was pretty much mimicking the way Kyle had just said *Mom?* that told Kyle she wasn't

71

ready to ground him for the rest of his life. She said it with fun in her voice. It was almost as if she was used to Kyle by now, as if she was only half-concerned he wasn't home when he was supposed to be while the other half was wondering what sort of new adventure he and his pals were up to, that gave Kyle the guts to give it to her straight.

"I'm going to Roosevelt Island. I'll be home in two and a half hours."

"What?"

"Lucinda is leaving. Her mother is making her move unless we do something about it."

"Yes, Kyle. I know Lucinda is leaving. I saw the sign. I live across the street from the Winstons too, you know."

"But, Mom! I'm onto something!"

"A lead on a caper?"

"A lead on a *what*?"

"*Caper*, Kyle. *Caper*. If you're going to throw around hip, cool, private-eye lingo, your old lady can too."

"My old lady?"

"Excuse me, dear. I have to shift my shoulder holster. The barrel of my gun is sticking me in my ribs."

"Mom!"

"Kyle. Sweetheart. This is *their* lives. *Lucinda's* and her *parents'*. Not *yours*. Honey, it just isn't any of your business. And oh, by the way, I can't believe I'm having this conversation at six o'clock at night with the sun getting ready to go down, and my one and only son whom I love and adore is out somewhere on the streets of New York City all by himself talking to me on his cell phone telling me he's about to take a subway to an island in the middle of the East River so the girl who lives across the street doesn't leave town. Sorry about that last sentence, dear. But a mother doesn't stop being a mother even if she's the mother of a secret agent."

72

"Mom! I have to do this! I just have to! Something terrible happened to Lucinda's mom twenty-three years ago!"

"Only she won't tell anyone what it is."

"That's right."

"And someone else will. On Roosevelt Island."

"How did you know?"

"And it has to be tonight?"

"Tomorrow night's Harry Templeton's big celebration! I have to know before tomorrow night!"

"Is Harry Templeton the bad guy?"

"That's what I have to prove."

"Okay."

"Okay?"

"Okay," his mom said. "Be the knight in shining armor. Save your damsel in distress. But do it and be home before nine, or I'm walking across the street and having a heart-to-heart with Lucinda's mother myself."

And she clicked off.

No *"Good-bye!"*

No *"I love you."*

Nothing mushy-gushy.

Just a click.

Not that Kyle's mom was angry or upset. She was fine. Maybe even a little excited. You know, that Kyle had come clean. Not that Kyle's mom didn't know that Kyle had secrets, the same way she'd had secrets when she was his age. *Still* had secrets. Which was why she was so excited her son actually trusted her with *this* secret and figured the least she could do was trust him back.

Kyle?

Flabbergasted. Totally. Standing on Fifth Avenue hiding behind Fortitude with the streams of people passing and Kyle's mouth hanging open staring at his cell phone.

His mom had said, *"Okay!"*

"Okay!" she'd said.

Which sent a shot of guilt straight up his backbone. Because for a second—maybe even less than a second, maybe half of a second—Kyle felt happy. There's no other word for it. Kyle felt happy his mom and dad weren't living together. If they had been—if his mom and dad had never split—then Kyle and his mother would never have been forced to depend on each other the way they had the past few months. Which meant they might never have gotten to know each other as well as they had. Or trust each other. Enough so Kyle could tell his mom what he just told her and she could tell him okay. And don't think for a moment I'm saying that parents separating or getting divorced is a good thing. But there are times when maybe, just maybe, something cool might happen too.

"Ready?"

This wasn't Kyle's mom. She didn't call her son back with a vague, open-ended, follow-up question. This was Lucinda speaking from four steps above Kyle, her right shoulder leaning against Fortitude's hind leg, her left hand petting his tail.

"What about Ruben?" Kyle said.

But Lucinda didn't answer. Not right away. Instead, she hopped down the steps so fast that Kyle had to catch her to stop her from sailing into the street. And then she still didn't answer. Not until she looked up at him, smiled a smile Kyle had never seen before, and whispered:

"Who do you think told me to come?"

CHAPTER 14

And so they ran the long block west toward Sixth Avenue to catch the subway that would take them to Roosevelt Island. They sidestepped piles of plastic garbage bags. They zigzagged around oncoming pedestrians. They hopped over a stack of paperback books a woman was selling next to a fire hydrant next to a NO SOLICITING sign.

Was Lucinda afraid of losing Kyle?

Are you kidding?

She kept on his heels the whole way down the block until they reached the top of the subway stairs, where the riptide of New York commuters streaming up the steps forced Kyle and Lucinda to separate. Kyle hugged the right rail. Lucinda hugged the left. They inched their way down past that lovely urine smell into that hot, moist subway air, where Kyle stuck his hand inside his pocket and pulled out his subway card. He swiped it through one slot for Lucinda then swiped it through another slot for himself, and then he and Lucinda pushed through the turnstiles and ran like mad down the steps to the left because they'd just heard a train's brakes start to screech. And, yeah, it was the F train, but it was so crowded that there was barely any room to stand. Kyle and Lucinda had to jam themselves right up against each other. And if you think Kyle didn't like being jammed against Lucinda, you're crazy.

"How many stops before Roosevelt Island?" he shouted.

"Four!" Lucinda shouted back.

But those four stops suddenly turned into three. The F train screeched to a halt at Lexington Avenue and Sixty-third Street and didn't move. And the doors stayed open. And the folks inside Kyle and Lucinda's car started mumbling so loud Kyle couldn't make out the announcement over the train's intercom. Not that he would have been able to understand it anyway since no one in the history of mass transit has ever been able to understand anything anyone has ever announced over a New York City subway intercom. Except Lucinda. Which was another one of the many talents Lucinda had that Kyle didn't have a clue about.

"Tunnel's blocked!" she whispered. "No subway to Roosevelt Island! Let's get out of here before we're trampled to death!"

Lucinda didn't wait for Kyle to respond. She grabbed him by his forearm and pulled him out just ahead of the stampeding commuters. Only the harder Lucinda pulled the slower Kyle got until Lucinda wasn't so much pulling as dragging Kyle across the platform, up the steps, and out onto Lexington Avenue, where she turned and saw Kyle's face had gone white and his pupils were the size of a BB.

"What's wrong?" she said.

"I'm okay," Kyle said.

Yeah. Right. He was okay like Lucinda's mom was okay. Like everything was okay. This was the guy she was counting on? This was the guy who was going to stop her from moving to Atlanta? One minute she was leaping down the library steps and he was catching her, and the next minute he was shivering like a puppy because the tunnel was blocked and the subway couldn't make it to Roosevelt Island!

Wait!

Whoa!

That was it! The tunnel was blocked. So the only other means of public transportation that could get them to Roosevelt Island that evening was the tramway suspended two hundred and fifty feet above the East River by a wire. Which was cool. Way cool. Since it was maybe the best view of the city. Unless, of course, you couldn't look out the tramway windows because you were afraid of heights. Which Kyle was. Which Lucinda just remembered because she also just remembered the time when she was seven and Kyle was eight and they were on top of the jungle gym bars in the concrete park, and Kyle's face was as white as it was right now. Which was why it was a good thing that—just like every other subject in the world—Lucinda had read plenty about phobias. Which is a fancy word for fears. Ingrained fears. Deep-seated fears. The kind you can't explain.

Not logically.

You're just afraid.

The way Kyle was afraid at that very moment. He knew there were only two ways left to get to Roosevelt Island and one of them was a thirty-five-dollar taxi ride, which he knew he couldn't afford and doubted that Lucinda could either. So there'd be no taxi. Not tonight. Not with a measly ten-dollar bill in his pocket. But even though Kyle was sweating and turning pale and grabbing hold of his side because it hurt so badly, he wasn't turning around. In fact, he'd already started running again only this time straight for the tramway. And, yeah, Kyle may have been so scared he splashed right through a river of soapsuds and didn't even flinch when an old lady backed her wheelchair into his shin, but that didn't mean Kyle wasn't going to climb those zigzag stairs at Sixtieth Street and hop aboard that tramway and cross that river.

Why?

You know why. And so did Lucinda. Who suddenly realized she had a knot in her chest and pressure building in the back of her eyes. I'm not kidding. Wise guy, tough guy, cool guy Lucinda had turned herself into a sentimental basket case. Sure, she could have stopped it. But she didn't want to stop it. Kyle Parker was about to face down his fear for her. And she would have followed him anywhere. Even though, at that very moment, *he* was following *her* up that zigzag stairway, through that turnstile, and onto that tramway, where he stood in the middle, as far from the windows as possible, gripping a floor-to-ceiling metal pole. He gripped it so tight his hands went numb. But he didn't stop gripping it or open his eyes until the tramway jerked forward and Lucinda took hold of his hand.

The sun was going low behind the New York City skyline as Kyle and Lucinda glided along inside that floating skybox high above the East River on their way to stop twenty-three years of heartache and save Lucinda from leaving New York forever. Could it have been more romantic? Had there ever been a more perfect moment in the history of the world to kiss a girl? Was that what Kyle was thinking?

Nope.

His mind had zeroed in on the guy in the olive

raincoat leaning against the side of the tramway giving Kyle and Lucinda the once-over and the woman in pigtails pulling the same stunt, only she was checking them out with quick glances, on the sly, as if she was pretending not to check them out at all. You see, Kyle had always had an overactive imagination. And usually this overactivity focused on the dark clouds in the distance or the tunnel at the end of the light. I mean, here he was holding hands with Lucinda, but his mind kept flashing on Harry Templeton. Not that Kyle thought Harry Templeton was the guy in the raincoat or, of course, the woman in the pigtails. But could either one of them be a spy?

See?

Told you.

Overactive all the way. And, yeah, Kyle knew it was a long shot. And silly. And paranoid. And self-centered. And about a dozen other illogical terms and phrases he tried and failed to think of. Something—*anything*—to get him to stop thinking like a fool. But the voice in the back of his head kept whispering:

Twenty-three years. Harry Templeton has been guarding his secret for twenty-three years. And he's a thief and a liar. And he stole Lucinda's mom's career. And he scared her so much she's afraid to talk to her own daughter about it. Do you think he'd stop at a little spy work? Do you think Harry Templeton wouldn't want to check to see if anyone is visiting the guy who hired the woman whose career Harry Templeton stole on the night before his great big party to celebrate his triumphant return to New York?

A chill shot up Kyle's spine. The hair on the back of his neck prickled. Sure, sure. It probably had nothing to do with the man in the raincoat or the woman in pigtails. After all, Kyle had stared at people holding hands plenty of times, so what the heck? But, still, it was something. A guy like Harry Templeton didn't get where he got without watching his back.

Was he out there?

Waiting?

You bet he was. Kyle might not have known exactly where or how Harry Templeton would try to stop them. But Kyle knew this much. He knew if he and Lucinda kept going the way they were going they'd find out what Harry Templeton had in store for them, maybe even tonight.

Errrrrrr!

That was the tramway.

The car had begun its descent and was grinding to a halt at the Roosevelt Island station, but not before Kyle had talked himself into taking three deep breaths, then looking out over the trees and spotting what had to be the hospital compound no more than five hundred yards away on the southern tip of the island. And that was all Kyle needed. Before the doors had cracked open a foot, he hit the platform running, went straight down the ramp until he reached the crossroad parallel to the river, then cut left toward the hospital, leaving Lucinda no choice but to follow.

"You're probably wondering why I'm not upset you took the first opportunity that came along to quit holding my hand and start running," Lucinda said.

"No, I'm not," Kyle said.

"Well, you should be," Lucinda said. "You've been mooning after me for six straight days, wondering if I'd ever make up my mind between you and Ruben, and when I finally do and pick you, the next thing I know you're running away like you've just been forced to eat worms. So you better be wondering why I'm such a good sport and I'm acting like this is normal procedure, or I may go home right now and pack my bags and *beg* my mom to move to Atlanta."

Kyle stopped running and gripped the pain in his side and doubled over and gasped for air and kept gasping after he straightened back up and pretended not to notice that Lucinda had barely broken a sweat.

"I ran away because I got the creeps," Kyle said.

"Lovely," Lucinda said.

"Not about holding your hand. About Harry Templeton."

"Because he's a liar and a cheater and because the day before his great big party to celebrate his triumphant return to NYU he might want to send some spies out to check to see if anyone is going to the hospital to visit the man who hired the woman who never finished her dissertation?"

"Sounds stupid when you say it out loud."

"Maybe," Lucinda said. "But I was thinking the same thing."

Call it an epiphany.

Or let's just say Kyle finally realized that he and Lucinda were standing under a bridge. The Queensboro Bridge to be exact. Though the name of the bridge wasn't what made his shoulders shiver. It was the deserted, empty darkness that surrounded them. The streetlights were just blinking on. But the two closest were burned out. Which told Kyle that even if Harry Templeton wasn't lurking in the shadows, this wasn't exactly the spot a couple of kids wanted to be anywhere near after the sun went down.

Snap!

Whirrrrr!

Whisssssssssh!

The shadows from the trees and bushes danced on the concrete columns. The wind whipped off the water. The tires on the bridge droned way, way up above. I don't know which was the sound that spooked Kyle. Maybe all three. But he took off running again. Only this time he didn't leave Lucinda. This time he grabbed her hand and nearly jerked her arm out of its socket. Not on purpose. He was just revved up. Which Lucinda understood. Totally. Since her heart was now hammering as hard as his was.

Snap!

Whirrrrr!

Whisssssssssh!

Okay. Enough. The sounds were spooky, sure. But that was all they were. Sounds. They never turned into footsteps bearing down hard behind them or some creepy spy leaping out from behind a tree. No one was tailing them. Or, if someone was, he missed his chance to grab them where no one else could have heard them scream. Because Kyle and Lucinda were back in civilization. Too bad there wasn't an Olympic-sanctioned three-hundred-and-sixty-yard dash because these two would have shattered the world record. But that was all behind them. Kyle and Lucinda were now gulping down air at the edge of Glenmore Memorial's parking lot where everything checked out fine. Better than fine. Ordinary. As far as Kyle and Lucinda could tell, there wasn't a single thing strange about Glenmore Memorial Hospital except . . .

No one else was around!

I don't mean the hospital was deserted. People were there—in their rooms, in their offices, walking the halls, sleeping, eating, watching television, taking medicine. They just weren't anywhere near the main

entrance. There was no guard by the door. There was no receptionist behind the desk. What was the deal? Hospitals had staffs. People met you at the door, took your insurance cards, put you on gurneys, and rolled you into the emergency room.

That was it!

There wasn't any emergency room!

Kyle reread the name over the sliding glass doors. *Glenmore Specialty Hospital and Nursing Facility.* This was an old folks home! The kind of place where his dad used to work! Only this one wasn't in the Bronx. It was more upscale. The floors were cleaner. The furniture was newer. The air was fresher.

No.

That wasn't true.

The air still smelled like disinfectant and canned chicken soup. But the few times Kyle had visited his father in the Bronx after dark, the lobby was just as silent as this lobby was. Old folks in nursing homes went to bed early. And when they did the people who worked there disappeared to eat supper, play cards, watch TV, take a nap. In other words, visiting hours were over. Which meant Kyle and Lucinda couldn't be seen or heard, or they'd be kicked out. Which made things kind of difficult since Kyle didn't have a clue how to find John T. Beecham's room.

"Over here," Lucinda said.

She said it so softly Kyle barely heard her as she tiptoed over to the reception desk, sat down on the chair, switched on the computer, and typed John T. Beecham's name in the box marked PATIENT.

"Three twenty-six," she whispered.

Easy as pie.

Easy as one-two-three.

Though Lucinda didn't gloat or pat herself on the back. She simply got up from the computer and said:

"Better not take the elevator. It'll make too much noise."

She pointed to the neon sign that spelled STAIRS above the door at the end of the hallway straight ahead. Perfect. No sweat. Nothing could stop them now. Nothing at all. *Except the lit, open doorway halfway down the hall!*

"Stay back," Kyle whispered.

"What are you going to do?" Lucinda whispered back.

"Find out if anyone is inside that office."

Kyle didn't wait for an answer. He moved. Slowly. Ever so slowly. He crossed the lobby, slipped along the wall of the hallway right up to the doorframe, crouched down on his knees, put his head next to the floor, and pushed forward out into the light.

Nobody!

Empty!

And maybe Kyle should have been pleased, since it meant he and Lucinda wouldn't have to sneak past. But come on! What was going on here? The place was like Dodge City the day after Pat Garrett and Billy the Kid left town. Kyle, however, told himself he had other things to worry about as he pushed himself back to his feet, waited for Lucinda to join him, then headed straight for the neon sign. And, yeah, they both did their best to keep cool on the outside, but you can bet that closed-off staircase did nothing to stop the pounding of their hearts. Because they could feel it. Something was about to happen. They weren't sure what, but they were sure that staircase was leading them right to it. Lucinda gripped Kyle's hand. Kyle gripped Lucinda's hand. They tiptoed past the second floor. They tiptoed past the landing between floors. They kept climbing.

And climbing. Until there were only seven steps left.

Six.

Five.

They saw the crack of light underneath the door.

Four.

Three.

They gripped each other's hand tighter.

Two.

One.

Kyle grasped the doorknob, and pushed as hard as he could. If someone was on the other side, let him take it on the chin. But no one was. The third-floor hallway was as empty and silent as the office, the reception area, and every other place Kyle and Lucinda had passed inside and outside Glenmore Memorial Hospital that Friday night.

No.

Wait a minute.

Empty, yeah. But not silent. Kyle heard a sound. So did Lucinda. And not just any sound. But a voice. Soft at first. Then growing louder. And louder. Spilling out of one of the rooms. Kyle checked. Lucinda stuck her head out into the hallway and double-checked. There was no doubt about it. The shouting could only have been coming from one room.

Room 326.

CHAPTER 15

Inch by inch, they crept along the hallway under the glare of those bare, buzzing florescent bulbs. Ninety feet in front of them, the door to Room 326 was slightly ajar. That was why Kyle and Lucinda could hear the shouting. But it wasn't the only reason their mouths had gone dry and the hair on the back of their necks had turned to pinpricks. It was because the hallway was empty. There were no cleaning carts to hide behind, no nursing stations to duck under. If anyone walked out of that room, Kyle and Lucinda would have been busted.

"It's John T. Beecham," Lucinda whispered.

"You're sure?" Kyle whispered back.

"I recognize his voice. Only I've never heard him shout before, so it took me a second to realize it was him."

"I don't know what you're talking about!" John T. Beecham's voice exploded into the hallway. *"I've never discussed your precious* Receptor-Lock Key *article! Not with Loretta Winston or anyone else! Now leave me alone!*

Do you hear me? Stay away! Don't you dare step one foot inside this hospital or I'll call the police!"

Slam!

That was the sound of John T. Beecham's telephone crashing into its cradle. But, to Lucinda, it was more like a bell at the start of a horse race. She quit inching down that hallway and bolted for the door.

"Dr. Beecham!" she cried. "It's me! Lucinda Winston! I—"

That was as far as Lucinda got before she burst into John T. Beecham's room and saw his wrinkled, beet-red face look up from his three pillows and heard the vacuum bands wrapped around his ankles expand and contract to keep the blood pumping through his legs.

"Lucinda! Dear!" John T. Beecham cried. "You can't stay! He's coming! Harry Templeton is—"

Now it was John T. Beecham's turn to stop in mid-sentence the moment he saw Kyle follow Lucinda through the open doorway. John T. Beecham was expecting someone else, of course. Even though it was only five seconds since he slammed down the phone, he was expecting Harry Templeton. You could see the relief in John T. Beecham's bloodshot eyes. The relief didn't last, however. He was too wired. His hip was in too much pain. And if his head hadn't been propped up by those three pillows, the poor guy might have gotten whiplash his emotions were bouncing back and forth so fast.

"That was him!" he cried. "That was Harry Templeton! He was calling from his cell phone! His cab was pulling up to the entrance! You must leave! You can't be caught here!"

Ding!

The elevator.

Harry Templeton had arrived. Kyle and Lucinda

could hear his footsteps. But here's what's crazy. John T. Beecham didn't freak out. I swear! Up until this point, he'd been this old guy on this hospital bed with these wisps of white hair peeking out of his light blue hospital gown and his eyes all wild and his voice totally spooked. But the moment he heard the *Ding!* and realized Harry Templeton was getting off the elevator and headed this way, John T. Beecham's eyes went clear, as if he'd suddenly reached a decision.

"You can't leave," he whispered. "Not now. He'll see you. So it's into the bathroom, you two. I share it with Mr. Cunningham in three twenty-four. But don't slip out Cunningham's side and make your getaway until we find out exactly what this crook is up to and I send you the signal."

"The signal?" Lucinda whispered.

"You'll pick it up," John T. Beecham whispered back.

All those years Lucinda had known John T. Beecham. All the times he'd found her in her mom's office or the biology lab and offered her one of those root beer hard candies he always carried in his pocket. All the times she'd said no thank you, she hated root beer. All the times he'd answered that no one hated root beer. She'd always thought he was so old he couldn't remember they'd had this same conversation a hundred and fifty times. But he had remembered. He'd been teasing her. For years. He was *still* teasing her. Now! With Harry Templeton's footsteps echoing down the hallway!

The turnaround in John T. Beecham's personality was so surprising that neither Kyle nor Lucinda focused on the fact that their hiding place was a nursing home bathroom shared by two old men, especially after Harry Templeton burst into the room, put his hands on the metal bar on the side of the bed, and leaned over an inch away from John T. Beecham's face.

"Let's cut right to it!" Harry Templeton said. "Either Loretta Winston told you what happened with her dissertation or you worked it out yourself! Ahh! Don't play that game with me! You would never have hired her! Not even you! Not without her PhD! You think that's funny? You think this is a joke? Hey! I'm talking to you! You old softy! You old has-been! Lying there with those rubber bands wrapped around your ankles!"

Did Lucinda expect John T. Beecham to flinch?

Sure.

You bet.

Wouldn't you if you were flat on your back helpless in some hospital bed and some nasty creep got right up in your face? Not John T. Beecham, though. Not as far as Lucinda could see. In fact, as she peered through the crack in that bathroom door, she was sure she saw John T. Beecham's eyes actually sparkle.

"Is this a confession?" he said. "Are you saying you stole *The Receptor-Lock Key?*"

"I'm saying I don't like taking chances!" Harry Templeton said. "I'm saying I've waited long enough to find out what you know and if you have any proof to back it up! So tell me! Now! Or I may just go over there and lean on your brand-new hip!"

"No!" John T. Beecham cried.

"You think begging is going to help?" Harry Templeton said.

"Please!" John T. Beecham shouted. "Stay out of my office! Keep away from my desk!"

CHAPTER 16

John T. Beecham didn't just shout these last few sentences. His body started shaking, and the back of his head began banging against the three pillows as if he was in the middle of some kind of fit. The combination looked terrifying. But Lucinda didn't rush in and give him mouth-to-mouth resuscitation nor fling open the bathroom door and kick Harry Templeton in the shin. She'd given her word to John T. Beecham, and she wasn't about to break it. Because this was the signal. This was what she'd been waiting for. This was John T. Beecham's way of telling Lucinda where to go and where to look.

Kyle?

Confused.

He didn't understand why Lucinda wasn't screaming for a nurse instead of grabbing him by his T-shirt and pulling him out of the bathroom through the opposite door and right by Mr. Cunningham. Who, by the way, happened to be awake. And who also happened to have wisps of white chest hair peeking out through his light blue hospital gown. Kind of an old man thing, I guess.

Though his expression certainly wasn't. His face lit up with this great big grin as if he were thinking, *Okay! Finally! It's about time things started hopping around this joint!*

And then he was gone.

Or, at least, Kyle and Lucinda were gone. They were out the door to Room 324 and down that empty hall like a pistol shot. Kyle didn't bother asking any questions. He knew Lucinda was too pent up with excitement to give him any kind of an answer. He just did his best to keep up as she tore down the stairs, hit the ground floor running, and dragged him through those sliding front doors, heading straight for the taxicab parked in the circle with the motor running and the cabby lounging behind the wheel fixing a fishnet over his jet-black hair.

"No!" the driver shouted. "All taken! Full up!"

Did that stop Lucinda?

You've got to be kidding. Lucinda was a city girl. Manhattan was in her blood. You don't get in the way of a New York native and a taxicab, not if it isn't moving and the door isn't locked and the backseat isn't already crammed with three muscle men or an old lady and her poodle.

"It's okay!" she said.

And as she said it, she grabbed the handle and opened the door and shoved Kyle in and piled in next to him and kicked off her sneaker and lifted the insole and peeled out a hundred-dollar bill.

"Yours!" she cried. "All yours if you take us to 29 Washington Place in Greenwich Village!"

The taxi was waiting for Harry Templeton. That was what Lucinda figured. The same way she figured that this was the cab that brought him here, and when it arrived he told the driver to wait fifteen minutes and there'd be a good tip in it for him. That was why

Lucinda fished out the hundred-dollar bill her father had given her and told her to always keep it in her shoe for emergencies. Lucinda figured a hundred dollars for a forty-dollar taxi ride would be enough to make the driver forget his deal with Harry Templeton.

And she was right.

Max Wolf—that was the name on the cab driver's permit on the dashboard next to the glove compartment—didn't hesitate. He punched the meter, stepped on the gas, pulled the wheel hard, and burned rubber pealing out of that Glenmore Memorial Hospital parking lot.

"He was talking to me!" Lucinda shouted. "John T. Beecham was talking to me! All that flopping around on the bed? That was for me! That was his signal! He was telling me to go to his office! He was telling me to check his desk!"

Did it occur to Lucinda that John T. Beecham was also telling Harry Templeton the same thing?

Think about it:

No matter how much John T. Beecham's words may have sounded like babbling from a guy who'd just blitzed out, there was no way Harry Templeton could afford *not* to check out what John T. Beecham just said. And maybe Harry Templeton had already discovered his taxi wasn't waiting for him and dialed the dispatcher. Which meant what? Lucinda and Kyle had a fifteen-minute head start?

Ten-minute?

Five?

Though Kyle wasn't thinking about Harry Templeton. He was caught up in the cab ride. Or maybe I should say *flight*. Because there are taxi drivers, and there are *taxi drivers*. None drive slowly, not if they're New York taxi drivers. But every once in a while, you run across a lunatic like Max Wolf. If there was an inch between his front bumper and the rear bumper of the car ahead, that was a half-inch too much. Same deal with an opening in the lane next to him. In-out! Up-back! Though when I say *back*, I don't mean Max shoved the cab into reverse. It just felt like reverse when he slammed on the brakes and a Hummer shot past close enough to feel the slipstream.

You see guys in stock car races. They cut in. They cut out. They ride bumpers. They take turns faster than a rocket ship. But that's without red lights and oncoming traffic and old ladies going thirty-five and kids throwing buckets of water at passing cars then volunteering to wash the windshields. But let me say this. Max Wolf was a pro. I'm not saying there wasn't plenty of daredevil and wild man underneath that fishnet of his, but he was also a pro. He had to be, or he wouldn't have still been alive to enjoy the panic on Kyle's face in the rearview mirror every time Max pulled the wheel or punched the accelerator.

Though maybe Kyle's panic also had something to do with what he was hearing. Maybe he'd sorted out just enough of what Lucinda had just told him to realize her plan included the two of them breaking into John T. Beecham's office in the NYU biology building and grabbing whatever was hidden in John T. Beecham's desk and beating it out of there before Harry Templeton caught them and swiped back whatever they found and maybe pushed them out a window for good measure. Or maybe Kyle was thinking none of those things. Maybe he was simply wondering how Lucinda figured she'd even be able to make it inside John T. Beecham's office in the first place.

"You're wondering how we're going to make it inside John T. Beecham's office in the first place," Lucinda said. "Which means you've forgotten I know everything about locks. Remember? It's how we broke into your dad's desk last year. But what you don't remember— what you couldn't remember since I never told you— was the guy who lent me the book on locks was John T. Beecham. Which is another reason I know he was talking to me back at the hospital. Because he knows I can pick locks. Because he knows I can pick his *office* lock. The day I gave him back his book, he locked himself inside his office and waited while I opened the door."

Errrrrrrrrr!

This was the cab's brakes. Fortunately, it didn't mean they were headed for a fire hydrant or a head-on colli- sion. It was just Max Wolf's way of ending a trip. His signature, so to speak. The taxi was pulling up in front of 29 Washington Place, and Max was giving it one last fishtail.

Errrrrrrrrr!

Kyle's forehead clanked against the Plexiglas barrier separating the backseat from the front seat. His lips mashed against the scratched surface. Perfect. Very cool. Especially since Lucinda's head barely even bobbed as she balled up the hundred-dollar bill, tossed it through the opening in the Plexiglas, jerked open the back door, and gently—very gently—helped Kyle onto the curb.

"You're a very bad driver, Mr. Wolf," she said.

Lucinda didn't wait for an answer. She ran up the stairs and pushed the metal bar on the wooden double doors with her hip, turned back to Kyle climbing up the stairs behind her, and nodded once. The nod told him they were in. The doors to the building were unlocked.

"Okay," Kyle said.

"Okay what?" Lucinda said.

"Let's find it," Kyle said.

But first they had to pass the human skeleton and

brain floating in formaldehyde on that first floor while every car skidding to a stop and car door slamming and leather sole scraping the sidewalk reminded Kyle just how close Harry Templeton could be.

Thump!

Errrrr!

Whish! Whish! Whish!

None of these sounds signaled Harry Templeton's arrival. They were the sounds of the metal door at the top of the stairs after Lucinda's shoulder collided with that bar and the hinges creaked open before Kyle's and Lucinda's shoes raced down that empty second floor where Lucinda stuck her hand inside her pocket, pulled out the paperclip she always carried, slipped the straight end into the lock on the door to Room 214, twisted it clockwise, jerked it up, heard the *clink*, turned the knob, and they were in.

Just like that.

No problem.

Except for the ten zillion books and journals and papers piled all over the floor, the tops of the two metal filing cabinets on either side of the window, and across every inch of John T. Beecham's gigantic wooden desk. It was like a cyclone hit the place. No way were Lucinda and Kyle going to find what John T. Beecham had hidden and make their getaway before Harry Templeton arrived.

Or, at least, that was the way Lucinda saw it.

Kyle?

He saw it differently. In fact, he didn't see anything at all. It was more like he felt it. Or sensed it. The bottom of the desk, I mean. It was like it was calling to him, reminding him that what you *can't* see is sometimes more important than what you *can*. And so, without a word, he zigzagged around those books and journals and stacks of papers, ran his hand underneath the desktop, felt the envelope taped to the oak veneer, pried the tape loose, pulled the envelope away from its hiding place, tore the thick yellow paper along the back seal, pulled out the two pages so fast he nearly ripped them in half, and started to read out loud:

Dear Sir or Madam:

If you are reading these words, I have either instructed you where to find this letter or you are following the directions I have left behind in my safe-deposit box after my death. Either way, you are about to discover information I should have revealed in 1983. Harry Templeton did not discover The Receptor-Lock Key. *That discovery was made by Loretta Winston while she was a graduate student at New York University from 1980 to 1983. How can I prove this? I can't. Harry Templeton destroyed all of Ms. Winston's work before he published* The Receptor-Lock Key *under his own name. But I was present in 1983. I visited the lab often and witnessed firsthand who was putting in the hours and performing the experiments. My only explanation for my silence up until now has been my cowardice. Any accusation by me would simply have been my word against a man in possession of all the evidence, a man who would have stopped at nothing to ruin my reputation and my career. So I kept quiet. And for that I feel ashamed. But my feelings are not important here. Justice is. I am not—nor have I ever been—partners with Loretta Winston. I have never discussed my suspicions with her. She in no way has prompted me to make this confession. I have either finally found the backbone to call Harry Templeton the thief and the liar that he is, or I have gone to my cowardly grave and am well beyond the reach of one of the most treacherous scoundrels in modern science.*

Sincerely,
John T. Beecham

Kyle looked at Lucinda. Lucinda looked at Kyle. They were just about to throw their hands up in the air and high-five each other when they stopped. They froze. At the sound of the metal door opening at the top of the stairs.

Errrrr!

17

Fifty yards separated the steel door at the end of the second-floor hallway from John T. Beecham's office, and Harry Templeton had already covered five of those yards with his long, deliberate steps.

Clomp!

Clomp!

Clomp!

Clomp!

Clomp!

That meant what? Kyle and Lucinda had twenty seconds before Harry Templeton arrived? Twenty-five? Not a lot, that was for sure. Plus, there was no place to hide. They could have ducked behind John T. Beecham's desk, but it was open in the front. And don't think they could have slipped into a closet because there wasn't any closet. There weren't even any drapes to pull in front of them. There was just the room. The *open* room. Kyle and Lucinda were caught.

Unless . . .

Lucinda slammed John T. Beecham's door shut, slid the paperclip back inside the lock, twisted it counterclockwise, and held it there as tight as she could, locking them inside John T. Beecham's office.

Clomp!

Clomp!

Clomp!

Clomp!

Clomp!

Harry Templeton was moving faster now. Kyle could hear his footsteps coming closer and closer, and there was nothing he could do about it.

Clink!

That was Harry Templeton slipping a key inside the lock—the same key he probably just forced John T. Beecham to give him. Or, at least, that was what Kyle and Lucinda were telling themselves. Not that they really cared where Harry Templeton got the key. They were too busy listening to the pounding of their hearts as they waited to see if Lucinda's counterclockwise paperclip would keep Harry Templeton out.

Clink!

Clink!

No *Click!* The knob didn't move. Lucinda held on tight. It wasn't easy. The paperclip dug into her hand. But the paperclip held. The lock stayed locked.

Clink!

Clink!

That didn't mean Harry Templeton was about to give up. He wasn't deaf. He could hear Kyle and Lucinda shuffling around on the other side of the door. Harry Templeton knew someone was inside John T. Beecham's office. And Harry Templeton wasn't about to quit without a fight. He kept twisting his key, pushing hard, gaining leverage, feeling the key move as the lock started to give.

"Thirty seconds," Lucinda said.

"Huh?" Kyle said.

"Twenty-five!" Lucinda said.

It was then Kyle saw the paperclip moving in Lucinda's hand and instantly understood what Lucinda was saying. Pleading really. Not with her voice. Her voice could have been ordering a vanilla shake it stayed so steady. But her eyelids were pulling back inside their sockets. Kyle didn't blame them. He would have hid too if hiding had been an option.

But it wasn't.

And Kyle was wasting precious time thinking about eyelids and eye sockets. But not that much time. And, anyway, concentrating on seemingly unimportant details sometimes isn't all that bad an option.

It expands the mind.

It keeps it loose.

Loose enough in this case for Kyle to remember that most windows in New York City had fire escapes.

Bingo!

Kyle unlatched the lock and lifted the window and peered out and saw the steel staircase and hopped onto the window ledge and grabbed the opposite side of one of those metal filing cabinets. He performed all of these actions so quickly he didn't have time to think the rest of it through, so he just pictured it like a movie, fast-cut to increase the suspense. He'd shout "Go!" Lucinda would take three steps and dive through the window. The door would fling open. Harry Templeton would rush in. But Kyle would already have blocked the path.

Did he explain this to Lucinda?

No.

He didn't have to. Something about the way she looked at him told him she already knew exactly what he was thinking. In fact, Lucinda didn't even wait for Kyle to shout, "Go!" She just went. The momentum carried her over the window ledge and onto the landing where she rolled, released the catch to the fire escape stairs, then skipped the stairs altogether and slid down the rail.

Which meant she missed Kyle's best move, the one he thought of the instant he realized they could, indeed, escape but only if he made sure Harry Templeton couldn't follow. That was why Kyle grabbed that filing cabinet and waited while Harry Templeton turned his key one last time and flung the door open and made a grab for Lucinda's disappearing sneaker as she dove out the window. And then Kyle didn't wait any longer. He yanked!

Hard! Then he listened to the racket as the filing cabinet came crashing to the floor right in front of the window. It was a move that left Harry Templeton no option. He had to stop. He had to pull back. And all he could do was stare—or glare—at the back of Kyle's head as he disappeared down those fire escape stairs.

CHAPTER 18

"No!" Lucinda's mom said. "I won't do it! I won't let you go public with John T. Beecham's letter!"

"But *Mom*! Lucinda said.

"Don't *Mom* me!" Lucinda's mom said. "I'm not the one who arrived at her house at eight forty-five without calling her parents to let them know she hadn't been run over by a taxi. But we'll talk about family rules and consideration of others after Kyle goes home and skip right to the part that concerns you both. Sit, Lucinda. You too, Kyle. And calm down. We'll all try to calm down. And I'll try to explain why I refuse to take advantage of my boss's most generous offer."

And so they sat.

And took a deep breath.

Then another.

"I'm not being noble," Lucinda's mom said. "I'd use the letter if it were proof. But it isn't. The letter itself states that it isn't. And so it won't solve the problem. It will only turn a fine, honorable man who has already done more for me than I can ever repay into a laughing-stock. No one will believe him. No one will even take

what he has written seriously. Too many people over too long a period of time have had too much at stake in the supposed breakthrough of the great Harry Templeton."

Lucinda's mom pushed herself out of her beige chair, walked around the glass-topped table, sat down on the couch between Kyle and Lucinda, and took hold of both of their hands.

"Listen, you two," she said. "I'm touched. Though I can't say I approve of your shenanigans this evening, you certainly have shown me how much it means to both of you that Lucinda stays in New York. So I suggest a compromise. You give me your word that John T. Beecham's letter never goes public, and I'll give you mine that from now on I will no longer take the coward's way out. Twenty-four hours from this very moment, I will confront Harry Templeton. And then I promise you both, Lucinda will never have to leave New York. Not on my account."

Can't beat that, right?

Kyle and Lucinda must have flipped. Her dad must have hopped out of his chair and joined in the fun. Except there wasn't any fun. Lucinda's mom's words might have sounded light and carefree, but they couldn't hide the shadow that crossed over her eyes. Oh, she tried. She tried to blink it away and smile her brightest smile. But her lips went tight, and when she bent over to kiss Lucinda's forehead, Lucinda could feel them quiver against her skin.

"Great, Mom! What a relief!"

"Yeah, Mrs. Winston!"

"Wonderful news, dear."

That was how bad things were. Neither Lucinda nor Kyle nor Lucinda's dad could even call Lucinda's mom on her phoney-baloney happy face. Yes, she was going to finally stand up to Harry Templeton.

And that was good.

But nothing had changed.

Her mom still had no proof.

Sure, she might stop John T. Beecham from ruining his career. But, instead, Professor Winston was going to ruin hers. Lucinda even knew when and where this self-destruction would be taking place. Her mom had told her. Twenty-four hours from now was Harry Templeton's celebration at the Museum of Natural History. Which meant her mom wasn't only going to destroy her career. She was going to destroy it in front of every molecular biologist in New York City.

Lucinda didn't figure out this last part right there on the spot.

She was too shook up.

No, it was worse than that.

Lucinda was numb.

It was as if all of her sensory perception had shut itself down. She no longer felt her mom's touch or heard her mom's voice or even remembered saying good night to Kyle. After her mom's tight, quivering lips brushed against Lucinda's forehead, Lucinda felt nothing and heard nothing and remembered nothing until seven and a half hours later when she woke up in her bed in the dark with 3:35 a.m. glowing at her from her alarm clock on her nightstand.

"We've got to stop her!"

Lucinda whispered these words into the darkness. I can't tell you how her brain snapped out of its trance. I'm not sure if everything became crystal clear the moment she opened her eyes or if it had been a gradual process during her dreams.

No matter.

Lucinda was Lucinda again.

Sharp.

Determined.

Furious.

Yes, furious. It had been bad enough when all of this had been about her—*Lucinda*—and how she'd have to leave New York and Kyle and the secret agents. But that wasn't it anymore. Her mom had promised. Lucinda wouldn't be leaving anywhere or anyone.

But at what price?

Even without her PhD, Professor Winston was known as one of the best and brightest researchers in the country. But if she accused Harry Templeton of being a thief at the Museum of Natural History, he'd crush her. Lucinda wouldn't be moving to Atlanta. But not because her mom had decided she didn't want to go. Lucinda wouldn't be moving because Emory University wouldn't be hiring her mom as a professor. No one would. Plus, NYU would fire her. Harry Templeton would fire her personally. Tomorrow night! In public! Lucinda's mom would be out of a job forever. She might never be able to do research in a laboratory again.

"Is that you, Kyle?"

Oh, yeah.

I forgot to mention that while Lucinda was getting furious and whispering into the darkness and beginning to feel the first pangs of panic, she was also speed dialing Kyle's cell phone. Though that wasn't why she'd said, "Is that you, Kyle?" with such surprise in her voice. Her clock radio now read 3:36, but Kyle hadn't taken forty-five seconds to answer. It was more like two. And his voice wasn't groggy. It was alert. Wired even. As if he'd been waiting all night for her to finally call.

"Your mom said twenty-four hours," Kyle said without saying hello. "That means tonight. That means your mom is going to stick it to Harry Templeton in front of all those people at the Museum of Natural History but without any proof, so Harry Templeton is going to stick it to her right back."

"So why do you sound so excited?"

"Because your mom said we couldn't go public with John T. Beecham's letter. She didn't say we couldn't use it."

"What are you saying?"

"I'm saying I've been up all night Googling Harry Templeton. And check out his quote from *Newsweek* on April 22, 2001: 'I fly to London every October to get my suits handmade on Seville Road for twenty-five hundred dollars. Why? Because I can.' Here's another from *Time* on March 2, 2002: 'No, it's not easy keeping my mustache this precise. It takes thirty minutes a day. But when I see my photograph in your magazine, I'd say it's worth it. Wouldn't you?'"

"I don't get it," Lucinda said.

"Then try this one," Kyle said. "*People*, January 15, 2004: 'I trust no scientist anywhere at any time. How can I? They all want to be me.' Or the *Washington Post* on September 14, 2005: 'Of course I want to cure cancer. I may get it someday.'"

"So there's no one in the United States more self-centered," Lucinda said. "So what?"

"So I've already called Chad, Tyrone, and Ruben," Kyle said. "The secret agents are meeting at the Tofu Tutti-Frutti at ten a.m. sharp."

Tyrone's parents owned the Tofu Tutti-Frutti. That's why the secret agents started meeting there last year, not because it looked like a slick, sleek, silver caboose. On the outside, I mean. The inside looked like one of those old-time ice cream soda fountains with its Formica countertops and swivel chairs and stainless steel freezer compartments and chrome mixers and high-tech ice cream scoops. But the Tofu Tutti-Frutti had no soda. It had no ice cream, either. The specialty of the house was frozen chunks of tofu topped with unsweetened, heated carob sauce. Or, as Chad liked to call it, "A hot fudge sundae made out of Styrofoam and mud."

"Sorry I'm late," Tyrone said.

He said it sliding across the vinyl seat as he crammed himself into the back booth next to Kyle, who crammed himself against Lucinda, who crammed herself against the wall. The other side of the table had it worse. The other side had Chad. He sat on the aisle. Ruben sat next to the wall. If you could call it sitting. Ruben would probably have called it getting crushed to death.

"You're late, all right," Chad said. "Seven minutes and fourteen seconds! I'm not so sure you can just prance into a secret agent meeting any time you want and not get booted out on your butt. Shouldn't we discuss this or something? Debate the pros and cons? Vote by secret ballot?"

"If I were you, I wouldn't be all that quick to call for a vote on who should or should not be a secret agent," Ruben said.

"What's that supposed to mean?" Chad said.

"I bet even you can figure that out," Tyrone said.

"Oh, yeah?"

"Yeah!"

"Oh, yeah?"

"Yeah!"

Sound familiar?

It was like a playback of every secret agent meeting the secret agents ever had. With one slight exception. Chad. He finally woke up. Like a two-by-four smacked him across the forehead. Chad finally realized it was *him*. Against *him*. Everyone was always picking on *him*. Maybe it was because Tyrone still had some of those can-do vibes left over from his *acting in the theater of life* role yesterday at Lucinda's mom's laboratory that kept his voice steady and made Chad gulp. Whatever, Chad got it. He figured out the odds. Two against one. It was always two against one. And he—Chad—was always the one.

"I'm always the one!" Chad said.

"What are you talking about?" Tyrone said.

"Nothing!" Chad said.

"Good!" Kyle said.

Though the last thing Kyle was feeling was anything close to good. As you already know from his cell phone conversation with Lucinda at 3:36 that morning, Kyle had been up most of the night skimming those 2,567 hits on Harry Templeton that Kyle and Ruben had Googled earlier that afternoon. But lack of sleep wasn't the only reason Kyle's nerves were shot. Kyle was also scared.

Is that the right word?

Yes, I'm afraid it is.

All last night Kyle had been chock full of confidence over Lucinda actually holding his hand and the two of them racing to John T. Beecham's office, where Kyle had knocked over the file cabinet, assuring his and Lucinda's escape. They'd won! They'd outfoxed Harry Templeton! And the more Kyle read what a total, self-centered jerk Harry Templeton was, the more Kyle figured the secret agents could do it again. But that was six and a half hours ago in the safety of his bedroom, cherry-picking the websites and ignoring the part where Harry Templeton had, without a single drop of guilt, stolen Lucinda's mom's career. This was a ruthless man with a lot to lose, and the more Chad and Tyrone barked at each other across that Formica-topped table, the more it began to dawn on Kyle that getting a book published was nothing compared to facing down a man like Harry Templeton.

"We've got one chance," Kyle said. "We've got to make him confess."

"Confess?" Tyrone said. "You think Harry Templeton will confess?"

"Not in public," Kyle said. "Never in public. But Harry Templeton's a show-off. He'd love to confess. In private! Only in private! That's what I learned last night. That's what every article I Googled told me over and over again. He doesn't want to get caught. For sure he doesn't want to get caught. But Harry Templeton craves attention. There's nothing he'd like better than bragging about how brilliantly he pulled off the biggest scam in science history. Not to someone who could bust him. Just the opposite. He'd love to brag about his deep, dark secret, but only if he thinks it's safe. So that's exactly what the five of us are going to do. We're going to make him feel safe. We're going to make him feel invincible. Tonight, at his very own celebration, we're going to fake out the great Harry Templeton."

"Fake him out?" Ruben said.

"That's the plan," Kyle said. "Twenty-three years ago, Harry Templeton stole *The Receptor-Lock Key* from Lucinda's mom and claimed it was his own. He didn't hide what he stole. He wasn't ashamed of it. He rubbed Lucinda's mom's face in it. What does this prove about him? That he's a thief and a liar, sure. But it also proves that he doesn't care about anyone else. *What's in it for me?* That's Harry Templeton. That's what he lives by. It's not that he thinks of himself first then thinks of other people second. There is no second. It's him and only him all of the time. And if he thinks that way about himself, I'm betting he thinks that way about everyone else. I'm betting Harry Templeton believes that deep down inside *everyone* is only out for himself. How do you win a war? How do you beat the other team? You find the weak spot and attack. Harry Templeton is so self-centered he thinks everybody else is too. That's his weak spot. That's where we're going to hit him. That's how we're going to make Harry Templeton feel safe."

"What if he doesn't buy it?" Tyrone said.

"We'll make him buy it," Kyle said.

"How?" Ruben said.

And so Kyle told them. He told them all the details point by point, including the backup plan in case something went wrong. But forget it. I'm not running the whole thing down for you.

No way.

It would kill the suspense.

But I will tell you this. I will tell you what Kyle *didn't* tell them. He *didn't* say anything about John T. Beecham's letter. And Kyle certainly didn't mention that the letter wasn't really proof. Not in so many words. He and Lucinda had promised Lucinda's mom they wouldn't use the letter in public, and Kyle kept their promise.

Sort of.

Because Kyle assured the rest of the secret agents that he and Lucinda had found something in John T. Beecham's office that would make Harry Templeton chase after them. Even in a crowd. Even with hundreds of people around. And, yeah, it was a chance. Yeah, it was scary. But that was the thing about scary guys like Harry Templeton. You couldn't expect to trip them up without doing something a little scary yourself.

So there wasn't exactly what you'd call a pre-battle celebration in that back booth when Kyle finished explaining what the secret agents were up against. No high fives. No slaps on the back. The mood was so tense that Kyle may as well have spent the last forty-five minutes scraping his fingernails across the blackboard instead of weaving a delicate plot to stick it to Harry Templeton. Though that didn't explain Chad. Who, I swear, hadn't uttered a peep since he discovered everybody was always ganging up on him.

No bragging.

No obnoxious questions.

Chad stayed in that back booth just long enough to hear every word Kyle had to say, and that was it.

Chad split.

He squeezed out of the vinyl seat, marched across the black-and-white tile floor, and disappeared out the Tofu Tutti-Frutti front door.

"She didn't talk!" Kyle said. "She never opened her mouth! She barely even looked at me!"

Kyle hadn't flipped out. He wasn't hallucinating that Chad had suddenly morphed into a girl. Kyle was talking about Lucinda. That's right. You'd think Kyle might have been all whacked-out over Chad's sudden personality transformation.

But no.

Uh-uh.

Barely even registered.

It was Lucinda. All Kyle cared about was Lucinda. Who—if you recall—pulled practically the same stunt as Chad. Don't get me wrong. Lucinda didn't shove Kyle and Tyrone off that back booth's vinyl seat and stomp out the Tofu Tutti-Frutti's front door. She waited until the meeting broke up before she split. But that was just it. She left without a word. Leaving Kyle . . . Well, you know where it left Kyle.

Hurt!

Confused!

Furious!

Sorry about that last one. But what do you want from me? Kyle was a kid. He wasn't perfect. Here, he'd been up all night practically blinding himself on his computer screen, and when he finally hit on something that actually might work, what was the response from the girl he was trying to save?

Silence.

The cold shoulder.

The deep freeze.

Or, at least, that was the way Kyle saw it. And, yeah, Tyrone and Ruben might have seen it differently. But Kyle had no way of knowing that for sure since Tyrone and Ruben had already followed Kyle's instructions by taking off for the nearest Radio Shack. They had their assignment. Kyle had his. But before he headed uptown to case the Museum of Natural History so there'd be no screwups tonight, Kyle had to stop by Percy Percerville's. Because it was morning. Because that was what Kyle did every morning. He walked Shakespeare. He talked to Shakespeare.

Except this morning.

I'm not saying Shakespeare wasn't there. He was hopping up and down and licking himself and spinning in circles on Percy's reception hall marble floor in front of the bookshelves filled with sculptures of whales and bears and caribou and lots and lots of books. But Kyle wasn't talking to Shakespeare. Kyle was talking to Percy Percerville. Because Percy was part of Kyle's plan. Though Percy didn't know that yet. Though that hadn't stopped Kyle from promising the rest of the secret agents there'd be no problem. Percy would be more than happy to help. All Kyle had to do was ask.

"No," Percy said.

"No?" Kyle said.

"I believe that was my word, dear boy," Percy said.

opposite effect, but instead it made Lucinda realize that if her mom never did a single thing wrong then the confrontation with Harry Templeton at the museum tonight would be no big deal. Her mom would simply walk up to the man who had stolen all of her hard work and glory, tell him what was what, then walk away with her head held high. Now? Now Lucinda realized her mom was about to do exactly what Kyle had done back on the tramway. Her mom was scared silly, but she wasn't about to back down. Which, of course, was why the beauty Lucinda was seeing had a lot less to do with her mom's hair rinse than the look of determination in her mom's eyes.

All for what?

All for nothing.

Think about it:

Lucinda's mother may have been the bravest woman in Manhattan that Saturday night, but it didn't mean she wasn't going to destroy her career and take the secret agents and Percy Percerville down with her.

Yep.

You heard me. Percy was as good as his word. He'd promised the editor at Barcourt Publishers that Cynthia Marlow would appear at the Museum of Natural History that evening, and Percy had kept his promise. No, he wasn't wearing a dress and silly wig. He had on his usual red suit and black cape (with the red lining). Nor had Percy arrived by car to great fanfare under the floodlights and taken the celebrity march up the red carpet. Percy was on the sidewalk with the thousands of other fans jammed together outside the police barriers. Though, in Percy's case, *jammed* may have been stretching it since one glance at his outfit and the folks in his general vicinity didn't exactly crowd in tight, if you get my meaning.

Nor had Percy arrived alone.

He held his walking stick in his right hand and a leash hooked to Shakespeare in his left. And, as you might imagine, Shakespeare wasn't in any sort of a laidback mode. Not on that sidewalk with those TV cameras rolling and news announcers ready to pounce. Egged on by his master almost into a frenzy, Shakespeare started hopping. Up! Straight up! Four feet straight up and spinning three hundred and sixty degrees with every hop!

"Have you picked up her scent?" Percy cried.

"Arrr!" Shakespeare answered.

"Is it she?"

"Arrr!"

"The lady in the fake fur?"

"Arrr!"

"Don't play with me, Shakespeare! Don't toy with my emotions! No, you say? Not her? Not Cynthia Marlow? Not yet?"

You can imagine:

Every woman who stepped onto that red carpet got the same treatment. Percy would shout out his question. Shakespeare would yowl back his answer. And it wasn't long before all of the TV news crews quit training their cameras on the female professor-types arriving by the dozens. I'm not saying the roving anchors wouldn't have become more animated if the real, live Cynthia Marlow had finally made her appearance, but they had to admit that this crazy guy in the red suit and black cape carrying on a nonstop dialogue with his hopping dog wasn't the worst TV entertainment they'd ever experienced on a location shoot.

And that was before the secret agents arrived in a taxicab.

In style.

Not the taxicab. It was just a taxicab. The *oohs!* and

aahs! were saved for Lucinda's fancy-schmancy dress and Kyle's, Ruben's, Chad's, and Tyrone's tuxedos. (After all, this *was* a black-tie affair.) Which leads to the question: Where did these outfits come from? What kind of a high school kid ate a Tofu Tutti-Frutti hot carob supreme in the morning wearing blue jeans and a T-shirt then climbed the red carpet at the Museum of Natural History in an evening gown or perfectly tailored tuxedo at eight o'clock that night?

Friends of Percy Percerville, that's who.

Shakespeare's master wasn't the most successful romance novelist of all time simply because his sappy, sentimental plots could even make a football player weep. Nope. It was Percy's attention to details. The author of *Yes, Oh Yes!* and *My Amore Is Your Amore!* showed you a character's heart by describing his hat. Not just the color. But also the style, the designer, the *size*. One glance and Percy could calculate the height, weight, arm length, leg length, foot size, waist size, and neck size of anyone he ever met. Not close. Not within an inch or two. But an exact fit every single time! It was kind of a game with him, a game Kyle discovered at five p.m. that evening when one black, strapless, long dress and four tuxedos were hand-delivered to his front doorstep.

The result?

Stunning.

Percy had the same knack in real life as he had on the page. Nothing in those outfits bagged. Or bunched. Even Chad came off looking like he was . . . well . . . almost cool. Until, of course, he opened his mouth.

"Dig the crowd!" he said.

"They're not here to see you!" Kyle said.

He said it sharp.

Staccato.

He said it as if he were firing bullets at Chad instead of talking. Was Kyle suspicious? Hostile? Had he somehow discovered that his oldest friend had flipped over to Harry Templeton's side?

Nope.

It was nerves, pure and simple. Kyle was scared. Not of Harry Templeton. Kyle was afraid of failure. He was afraid his plan wouldn't work, and the secret agents wouldn't be able to bust Harry Templeton before he saw John T. Beecham's letter. Because once Harry Templeton realized there wasn't any proof, he'd know he was safe. He'd know neither Lucinda's mom nor the secret agents could touch him. So Kyle kept telling himself over and over again that the secret agents would have to move fast. Bait and switch. Razzle-dazzle. No time to sort it out or take it back. They had one shot and one shot only to make Harry Templeton come clean in front of witnesses. Not just the secret agents but also Harry Templeton's friends, the people he worked with, his fellow scientists.

That was why Kyle's plan had to be so exact. Picture Mozart creating a sonata or Michelangelo chiseling a block of stone. That was what Kyle was trying to do here. He was trying to focus on his plan, every detail, down to the spark of hate in Harry Templeton's eyes when he finally realized he'd been fooled by a pack of kids.

All of which Chad knew.

He knew how nervous Kyle was and how much this meant to him. So how could Chad walk up those steps next to his oldest friend with those flashbulbs flashing and those floodlights lighting up the sky? Because, remember, whatever happened tonight wasn't going to happen in a vacuum. The museum was a mob scene. There were hundreds of people. Thousands. With police everywhere. Some on horseback. The rest lining the barricades between the red carpet and the sea of adoring Cynthia Marlow fans. Especially one fan. Who—you've probably noticed—had taken a breather to let the secret agents soak up the spotlight.

But the breather was over.

Percy was about to snap back into action:

"No, Shakespeare! It can't be! Not her! Not this *girl*! Cynthia Marlow isn't a child! *Stop My Heart* and *The Devil's Moon* would have been written when she was minus two! Preposterous! I've never heard of such a thing! Did the newspaper lie? Have the TV stations played us for a fool? Wait, Shakespeare! There! Pulling up now! Oh, yes, it has to be! Oh, yes, it must!"

A limousine glided to the curb.

No.

Excuse me. A *1931 gold Pierce Arrow* limousine glided to the curb. And when I say *gold*, I don't mean the color of the paint. I mean actual gold bullion had been melted down and sprayed all over the entire exterior (with the exception of the sterling silver door handles, bumpers, hubcaps, and angel-winged hood ornament). We're talking one of a kind back in 1931, so you can imagine what that automobile would have been worth on today's open market.

You can imagine it.

Percy didn't have to.

He'd bought it four years ago from a pizza delivery entrepreneur who'd bought it from a smelting magnate who'd bought it from a railroad tycoon three months and two days after the final shot was fired in World War II. But Percy had never driven his prized possession. He'd kept it hidden in a garage on the Upper East Side waiting for the exact, right moment when the stage would be lit, the players would all be in place, and the thousands of people lining the sidewalk would scream and clap as the lead actor made his grand entrance.

His grand entrance?

That's right. Percy had always figured he'd be the actor. But that all changed the moment Percy had heard Kyle describe Lucinda's mom's showdown with Harry Templeton that evening, and suddenly all Percy could imagine was the Pierce Arrow glistening under the floodlights and the near pandemonium that was certain to break loose at the sight of Loretta Winston in her long, tight, black dress as she stepped out from the limousine's backseat.

How did Percy know what Lucinda's mom would be wearing?

He picked it out, of course.

As perfect as Tyrone had acted *in the theater of life* yesterday afternoon, that was Percy Percerville today. First and foremost, he was a writer. He knew a dramatic scene when it presented itself. But instead of typing it into his keyboard, Percy had written this one for real. He called his tailor. He called his chauffer. But, most important, he called Lucinda's mom and dad and set up a *"top secret, hush-hush"* meeting of the minds. And, yeah, I suppose I could tell you what they talked about, but I've got a feeling you've already sorted that one out for yourselves since eight hours later here they were, stepping out of that Pierce Arrow's backseat as grown men cried and women tossed flowers at Lucinda's mom's feet.

A college professor?

I don't think so.

Not to the folks behind those barricades. She was Cynthia Marlow. She had to be Cynthia Marlow. Who else would have arrived in a solid gold limousine, wearing a dress with a *V* cut down the back—*all the way down the back*!

"Oh!"

This was Lucinda. Who'd seen the makeover, of course. But the car? The dress? Uh-uh! No way! She was as dazed and bedazzled as everyone else. And it didn't end there. Not by a long shot. Because her mom didn't flinch. She didn't drop her eyes. She took Lucinda's dad's arm with her left hand and waved to the crowd with her right. Steel curtain? There wasn't even a hint of a steel curtain. Not even when the news anchors and their white-white teeth swooped in and shoved their microphones in Lucinda's mom's face.

"Are you—," started one.

"No comment," Lucinda's mom cut her off.

"But—"

"Sorry. I have nothing to say. Not at this time."

Was Lucinda's mom aware of the Cynthia Marlow scam? Was she being coy? Lucinda didn't know. She didn't care. She was too busy searching for Percy and Shakespeare. Who were gone. Vanished into the crowd. Which meant Cynthia Marlow had done her job. And now it was up to the secret agents to do theirs.

"It's time," Kyle said.

Time to get going. Time to set it all up. Time to quit gaping at Lucinda's mom's dress and wondering what she might say next. And so Kyle and Lucinda and Chad and Tyrone climbed the steps toward the museum entrance, and Ruben headed toward the Channel 13 van. That's right. Ruben didn't go inside the Museum of Natural History. Which, let's face it, seemed kind of nuts. I mean, here they were about to go up against Harry Templeton. Things could get rough. And the secret agents (minus Chad) could have used all the muscle they could get.

But remember. Ruben wasn't just a secret agent. He was also Ruben Gomez. A fact Kyle was counting on and the main reason he'd thought of the TV cameras in the first place. Ruben may have only been in high school. But he was still the star every New York sports writer dreamed of interviewing one-on-one. Which meant Ruben could go where no other secret agent could go. Ruben could get inside the Channel 13 van.

Why?

Good question. But if I answered it I'd be giving away too much of Kyle's plan. So instead we're going to follow the rest of the secret agents inside the rotunda. Not because they were on the move and the plan was about to unfold but because I don't want you to miss a single one of Chad's complaints.

"Do I really have to sit up front?" he said.

"How many times do I have to tell you?" Kyle said. "Yes. One of us has to be close to the microphone. So I picked you."

Chad said nothing.

Chad stomped off.

Not out of the museum. He actually did what he was supposed to do according to the plan. He walked ahead of his fellow secret agents, so it wouldn't seem as though they were together. Chad was supposed to pretend to be by himself. That way Harry Templeton wouldn't see Chad with Kyle and recognize him from last night and get suspicious. So, unbelievable as it seems, Chad not only stopped complaining but also stayed out front and led the way. Not right. Not toward the planetarium. Nor did he go straight toward the stuffed herd of elephants that looked as though they were about to trample anyone who didn't get out of their way.

Chad cut left.

He took the stairs down, past the hanging porpoise and octopus and giant squid and ten thousand other fish hanging from the ceiling or behind the glass cases or mounted on the walls. Only I'm not going to name them. I'm going to tell you about Lucinda. How she looked, I mean. I know I've already described the boys in their tuxedos and mentioned Lucinda's dress was strapless, but there was a lot more to that dress than no straps. Yes, it had a back. Nothing was going to steal Lucinda's mom's thunder. Though the combination of Lucinda's shoulders and face was so dazzling, a freelance photographer actually followed her inside the rotunda.

"You should be on the cover of *Cosmo*," he said.

"I'm in ninth grade," Lucinda said.

"Dig it," the photographer said.

"Dig what? Your grave?" Tyrone said.

As he said it, his lips twitched. Not in embarrassment. He wasn't backing down. He held the photographer's eyes, even though the photographer was a foot taller than Tyrone was. It was by far the most aggressive thing Kyle had ever heard Tyrone say to anyone other than Chad. So Kyle was confused for a moment. But then he got it. The tuxedo! Kyle realized Tyrone was using his tuxedo as a disguise. You know, for another part. An announcer at a boxing match? A gangster from an old black-and-white movie? No matter. It worked. It made Lucinda laugh. Out loud. And Kyle noticed she was laughing and realized it was the first time he'd seen her laugh all day.

Chad noticed nothing, of course. Chad turned right and left the hallway, and Kyle and Lucinda and Tyrone followed Chad under a hammerhead shark that guarded the room—the *gigantic* room—with yet another set of stairs. Only these stairs were open, zigzag, spilling out on what you were supposed to think was the bottom of the ocean.

If you looked up—way up—you saw a ceiling that looked exactly like the surface of the sea. If you looked around, you saw movie screens of porpoises and seals and walruses and sharks. If you listened, you heard whale calls that sounded like foghorns or Tibetan monks chanting. Which made sense. That you heard whales, I mean. Since right above you *was* a whale. A *blue* whale. The largest creature in the world. Not a photograph or a movie but an exact replica a hundred feet long hanging over you as if it were swimming through the air.

Oooooooooom!

OOoooOOOM!

Oooooooooom!

These were the sounds you heard. Mixed in with the sounds of the people. Six hundred? Seven hundred? Kyle wasn't counting. But he knew there were a lot. Plus there were all these waiters and bartenders and round tables filling up the floor. Most of the men were wearing old-time, beat-up tuxedos. Most of the women had squeezed themselves into the kind of a dress your mom probably wore to her prom. All were drinking wine or cocktails and trying to outtalk everyone in earshot and looking as if it should have been them and not Harry Templeton who was being honored tonight. I'm not saying these people weren't nice. I'm sure they were nice. I'm just saying that none of them was there for the reason he or she was supposed to be.

Creepy?

You bet.

A celebration honoring someone no one wanted to celebrate. You could tell. Or, at least, Kyle could. Though I wouldn't go patting him on the back since there wasn't anyone under that whale who was pretending anything else, certainly not after Professor Winston arrived at the top of those zigzag stairs with flashbulbs flashing all over the place.

A hush hit the museum.

Not just the whale room but all four floors. Even the piped-in *Ooooooooom! OOooooOOM! Ooooooooom!* shut up. The silence set the scene so dramatically that I wouldn't be surprised if Percy Percerville hadn't disappeared for this very reason—to bribe a guard to kill the sound system. Though the silence wasn't what caught Kyle's attention. His eyes were glued to Harry Templeton standing right next to the podium, wearing a tuxedo that was neither old-fashioned nor beat-up, pretending to listen to a woman who was pretending to congratulate him at the exact instant the hush hit.

But let me tell you something:

Harry Templeton may have been a thief and a liar, but he was also smooth. Someone else might have pouted or even stomped off in a huff when everyone's eyes shifted to Lucinda's mom at the top of those zigzag stairs. After all, this was supposed to be Harry Templeton's night. He was supposed to be the center of attention. But no dice. In that split second when everyone everywhere shut up and stared at the woman in the tight black dress and the flashbulb-popping paparazzi, even Harry Templeton must have realized that Professor Winston had stolen his thunder.

Or had she?

Sure, all eyes had shifted to her. And, sure, she knew how to tease those eyes into believing that if they left her for a moment they may very well miss the headline in tomorrow's newspapers. But, still, Harry Templeton didn't miss a beat. He was up those stairs and bowing at her feet and kissing her ring and taking hold of her arm as if *he* couldn't have been more excited she was there. That's right—*he*. Harry Templeton drew the attention back to *him*. Every bow and every kiss from Harry Templeton's lips all seemed to be saying the exact same thing:

135

"Yes, she's here. Some of you may know her as Professor Winston. Some of you may believe she's the woman the television newscasters are all calling Cynthia Marlow. And, yes, I understand you'd rather pay attention to her. And who can blame you? I'd rather pay attention to her too. But let's not forget something. Let's not forget why she's here. *Me!* She's here to see *me*. *I'm* the one who she's come to honor with her presence. *Me!*"

And man-oh-man was Harry Templeton pleased with himself. You could tell by the way he used the side (not the tip) of his index finger to smooth his paper-thin mustache. But then he stopped. Not just his index finger. His whole body went stiff. And white. The moment Lucinda's dad casually slid in between Harry Templeton and Lucinda's mom and took hold of her arm as if Harry Templeton hadn't been standing on the landing of the stairs at all. The move wasn't a threat. There was no face-off going on here. But at the same time Lucinda's dad was pretty much telling Harry Templeton that never in a hundred years would he be escorting Professor Winston down those zigzag stairs.

Lucinda?

She caught this little stairway drama, of course, but she was too busy trying to keep her knees from buckling to really appreciate it. Panic was what Lucinda was fighting. She'd been fighting it since she opened her eyes that morning. Panic was why she hadn't said a word to Kyle or even looked at Kyle at the Tofu Tutti-Frutti. Because it was one thing to worry about yourself. But it was another thing altogether to worry about someone else, someone you loved, especially your mom. And even from across the whale room with all those hundreds of people in between, Lucinda could tell by the way her mom's eyes were fixed forward that

nothing had changed. Her mom
down. She was headed straight
plugged into the podium that the a
were supposed to use to tell the wo
and brilliant Harry Templeton was.

But that was just it.

That was why the dull voice that ha
inside Lucinda's head all day had sudd
scream. Because no one had told her mom
after dinner when the secret agents were s
take their positions and the plan would be set.
mom was going to make her announcement no
dinner—without anything or anyone to back he

"NO!"

This wasn't Lucinda.

It was Chad.

He was on the speaker's platform screaming into
microphone and about to start screaming again:

"I'M TIRED OF YOU GUYS GANGING UP ON
ME ALL THE TIME! I'M TIRED OF YOU NEVER
LISTENING TO ANYTHING I SAY! AND NOW YOU'RE
ABOUT TO DO THE SAME TO HARRY TEMPLETON!
WHO'S A GREAT GUY! A COOL GUY! WHO NEVER
DID ANYTHING WRONG! BUT YOU DON'T CARE!
YOU'RE GOING TO ACCUSE HARRY TEMPLETON
OF BEING A THIEF BEFORE HE CAN EVEN DEFEND
HIMSELF!"

You can imagine the chaos. Some of the people started
shouting. Others were straining their necks.

Who was this kid?

Who was he pointing at?

Was it the other kids?

The kids in the back?

The crowd turned in unison. It was as if nothing else
existed inside that whale room except Kyle, Lucinda,

137

one. The people around them backed off. A circle
. Not big. But big enough so the folks up front
see their faces. Especially one of the folks. The
of the hour. Harry Templeton. Who saw, all right.
could tell the way his lips went thin the moment
aw that the kid with the cowlick was the same kid
h last night, the kid who climbed out the window in
n T. Beecham's office, the kid whose heart had just
bloded in his chest.

This wasn't the plan. This wasn't the way it was supposed to happen. Not now. Not until everything was set up. And, yeah, I know I said Kyle had a backup plan because he figured something would go wrong. But not this wrong. Not Chad screaming into the microphone and accusing the secret agents of being the bad guys. Kyle wanted to scream himself. He wanted to hop up and down. He wanted it to be two hours ago and have a chance to plan it all over again. But it wasn't two hours ago, and he didn't hop up and down or scream.

He ran.

Why?

Because he knew Harry Templeton would follow. Even with Chad screaming and all those hundreds of people watching, Harry Templeton would have no choice. He'd have to chase after Kyle because Harry Templeton couldn't risk letting Kyle get to the TV cameras because Harry Templeton didn't know that John T. Beecham's letter wasn't proof.

So Kyle took those zigzag stairs two at a time, shot underneath the hammerhead shark, sprinted past the octopus and giant squid, cut across the deserted Welcome Hall, grabbed the brass rail, and half-pulled/half-ran up that stairwell to the main floor. But he *didn't* race out the front door past the guard to the TV cameras. He kept climbing—his footsteps echoing off those marble walls—until he reached the third floor mezzanine of the African Wing that was shaped like a racetrack with a gigantic hole in the middle looking out over those charging elephants thirty feet below. Surrounding the hole was a four-and-a-half-foot concrete wall. Surrounding the opposite walls were glass display cases filled with stuffed cheetahs and chimpanzees and wild dogs and leopards. There were no corners. Nowhere for Kyle to be trapped. Not if he kept running next to that four-and-a-half-foot wall and, if he were fast enough, stayed out of the reach of Harry Templeton.

"Kyle Parker!"

There are probably worse things than having your name spoken by some old guy with a pencil-thin mustache who has just chased you up the stairs of the Museum of Natural History into a dark, deserted mezzanine surrounded by stuffed wild animals. At that particular moment, however, Kyle couldn't think of any.

"Yes, Kyle, I know your name!" Harry Templeton said. "I'll even tell you how I know it in a moment. But before we continue our pleasant little chat, I'd like you to rip off that hidden microphone you have taped to your chest."

Whoa!

So that was why the boys had gone to Radio Shack that morning and why Ruben had ducked into the TV news van this evening and why Kyle hadn't run out of the front door of the museum just now. Kyle was supposed to get Harry Templeton to confess he'd swiped *The Receptor-Lock Key* in a secluded spot where he thought only Kyle could hear, and Ruben and the Channel 13 engineers were supposed to make sure that everybody outside behind the barriers or downstairs inside the whale room could hear every word!

Only Chad had gone back to Serendipity.

Chad had cut a deal.

And now Harry Templeton knew the whole setup and was keeping his distance and talking just softly enough so the hidden microphone couldn't pick up a word he said. Which left Kyle two options. He could either do as he was told or walk away with nothing (which, of course, wasn't an option at all), so Kyle reached under his shirt and ripped off the microphone.

"Drop it!" Harry Templeton said.

Kyle dropped it.

"Stomp on it!"

Kyle stomped on it.

"Much better," Harry Templeton said. "Don't you agree?"

Kyle didn't answer. Partly because he wasn't sure if he could keep his voice steady but also because of the footsteps. Not Harry Templeton's footsteps. Different footsteps. A third person had entered the mezzanine. Kyle could just make out Chad's silhouette backlit by the neon EXIT sign over the mezzanine door. Only Chad wasn't turning right the way Harry Templeton had. Chad was turning left. Which meant the racetrack circle around the concrete wall was no longer open-ended. Chad had cut off Kyle's escape.

"Just give him what you got in Beecham's office," Chad said. "Who cares if Lucinda's mom came up with *The Receptor-Lock Key*? Big deal. You've got to take what you want in this world. No one's going to give you anything. You have to look out for number one."

"You just think of that?" Kyle said.

141

"Nope!" Chad said. "It was you. You're the one who gave me the idea this morning at the Tofu Tutti-Frutti when you said Harry Templeton was only out for himself. 'Why not?' I thought. 'No one else cares about me! Maybe it's about time I started caring about myself!' And so I went back to Serendipity. I told Harry Templeton about the hidden microphone. But not right away. Not until he told me I'm a lock on NYU pre-med."

"And there's no reason I can't cut you the same deal, Kyle," Harry Templeton said. "And not just NYU. I have contacts in every major university in the country."

"Because of Lucinda's mom's idea," Kyle said.

"*My* idea!" Harry Templeton said.

"So you admit she wrote it," Kyle said.

"I admit nothing!" Harry Templeton said.

And as he said it he moved in so close he could have lunged at Kyle. But Harry Templeton didn't. He waited. He bided his time. Why? Maybe because Harry Templeton liked to watch Kyle sweat. Or maybe because Chad hadn't made it around the mezzanine turn, and Harry Templeton wanted Chad to see.

"So now what?" Kyle said.

"What do you think?" Harry Templeton said.

"I think you're stronger than I am," Kyle said. "I think you're going to jump me and grab John T. Beecham's proof or toss me over the wall."

"Toss you over the wall?" Harry Templeton said. "Don't be ridiculous. I've no intention of tossing you over the wall. You'd take the proof over the wall with you. Your friend, on the other hand, wouldn't!"

Faster than you'd figure an old guy could lunge, Harry Templeton lunged. But not at Kyle. Who winced. You bet Kyle winced. And his joints locked. And his eyes bugged out of their sockets as Harry Templeton flew right past and grabbed Chad. That's right. Chad.

Who, by this time, had finally rounded the far turn and was now standing no more than five feet behind Kyle. A perfect lunging distance it turned out since Harry Templeton grabbed Chad by the lapels of his tuxedo and, in the same motion, leaned him over the wall.

"What are you doing?" Chad cried.

"Nothing personal," Harry Templeton said. "Think of yourself as a means to an end. My means. Your end."

"No!" Chad cried. "Kyle! Make him stop!"

"That's right," Harry Templeton said. "Stop me, Kyle. Hand over John T. Beecham's proof, and your friend won't have to impale himself on one of those elephant's tusks."

Did Kyle hesitate?

Even for a second?

Nope.

He slipped his hand under his cummerbund, pulled out John T. Beecham's letter, and held it over the wall. You heard me. He didn't hand it over. He didn't trade those yellow sheets of paper for his oldest friend's life. And, yeah, Kyle's heart may have been hammering like crazy and his mouth was so dry every word was followed by a click, but that didn't mean Kyle was about to back down.

"Admit it," Kyle said.

"Kyle!" Chad said.

"Admit Lucinda's mother came up with *The Receptor-Lock Key*, and I'll hand the letter over!"

"Hand it over *now!*" Chad said.

"What possible good would my admitting it do any of us?" Harry Templeton said. "I'd just call you a liar. I'd just say you're friends with Professor Winston's daughter and that you'd do anything to keep your friend from moving out of the city. You and I both know it would be some teenager's word against the word of a world-renowned scientist. Who do you think the world will believe?"

"You!"

Kyle didn't answer Harry Templeton. Lucinda beat him to it. Backlit by that very same EXIT sign, Lucinda walked out of the shadows. And maybe her heart was hammering as hard as Kyle's and her mouth was just as dry, but that was inside. Outside, she was Lucinda again. Outside, there wasn't the least bit of panic in her voice.

"The world will believe the great Harry Templeton," she said. "But this isn't about the world. It's about you. Over the past twenty-three years, you've probably talked yourself into almost *believing* my mother's theory is yours. Because you've never had to admit it to anyone. Well, that was the old deal. This is the new one. You've got to confess. You've got to say it out loud. If you do, Kyle will make the trade. My mother's career for Chad's life. Go on! Say it! Now! Before I push Chad over that wall myself!"

Perfect.

The setup was complete.

If Kyle was right and Harry Templeton was such a bragger and a show-off he was dying to tell someone safe how he'd pulled off the scientific scam of the century, Lucinda had given him the perfect opportunity.

Should I?

Shouldn't I?

That was what Harry Templeton's eyes were saying. His pupils were pinpricks. He squinted. Not because there was a sudden glare. Harry Templeton squinted because his fire and ice look was back.

"Twenty-three years ago, I ransacked your mother's cubicle," he said. "By the time I finished, there wasn't a single shred of evidence to back up any accusation.

144

How did I know this? Because I'd been in that biology building all night making sure that every scrap of paper with her name on it had been burned and that all documentation was now in my handwriting locked inside my safe! *I* was publishing *The Receptor-Lock Key.* That was what I told her. Not her. *Me!* And if I ever heard even a whisper that she was claiming any part to be hers, I'd brand her a thief and a liar, and I wouldn't stop until there wasn't a single soul left inside the scientific community who'd hire her even to mop the floor!"

"Say it!" Lucinda said.

"Say what?" Harry Templeton said.

"Say it's my mother's!"

"I thought I just did."

"Say the exact words!"

"It's hers. It's your mother's."

"What's her name?"

"Professor Loretta Winston."

"What did she discover?"

"The Receptor-Lock Key."

"Say it again."

"The Receptor-Lock Key."

"My mother, Professor Loretta Winston, was the one who discovered *The Receptor-Lock Key?*"

"Yes."

"Say it!"

"Professor Loretta Winston discovered *The Receptor-Lock Key.*"

"Say it again."

"Professor Loretta Winston discovered *The Receptor-Lock Key.*"

"Give him the letter," Lucinda said.

"You're sure?" Kyle said.

"Give him the letter!" Lucinda shouted.

So Kyle did. He dropped it. He dropped John T.

Beecham's letter. Not over the wall so it would drift down and lodge itself on top of the tallest charging elephant's back. Kyle dropped the letter at Harry Templeton's feet. Or Kyle tried to. Harry Templeton snatched the piece of paper in midair with his right hand and let go of Chad's lapel with his left.

But check it out:

Chad didn't run away or fall on his knees and start begging Kyle and Lucinda to forgive him for his treachery. Nope. Chad did something so uncharacteristically Chad that if Kyle and Lucinda hadn't been so intent on watching Harry Templeton's eyes gobble up every word of John T. Beecham's letter, the two of them might have fainted right there on the spot. *Chad simply stood there.* He took a deep breath. He crossed his arms. And, just as he did back at the Tofu Tutti-Frutti, he shut up.

"Wait a minute!" Harry Templeton cried. "This is all you've got? It's just a letter. It's just John T. Beecham's opinion! It isn't proof! It never was proof! You've got nothing!"

"Nothing?" Kyle said.

"Nothing!" Harry Templeton shouted.

Only this time when he shouted it, Harry Templeton's voice exploded from everywhere. It bounced off the ceiling, the walls, the floor, and then it came boomeranging right back at him.

And that was it.

That was when Harry Templeton finally got it. That was when he threw John T. Beecham's letter aside and saw that Chad had hitched up his right pant leg and that something was strapped around his sock. Something small. Something dark. Something that looked exactly like a microphone.

CHAPTER

24

No one saw Ruben duck out from the shadows behind the biggest elephant below and slip back outside to the Channel 13 News van. No one saw him. No one heard him. And no one but the secret agents even knew he'd been there. But he had been. Which meant Chad had never been in danger of ripping his guts out on those elephants' tusks. Sure, it was a long shot that Harry Templeton was crazy enough to toss Chad over that wall, but Ruben had it covered. Kyle didn't know how. Ruben didn't tell Kyle how. But if Ruben said he'd catch anyone thrown off the mezzanine, that was good enough for Kyle.

In other words, Kyle hadn't willy-nilly sent Chad out to be a double agent without backup. That's right. Chad had never been a traitor. He'd been following the instructions Kyle had given him back at the Tofu Tutti-Frutti and gone deep undercover. So deep, in fact, that Kyle wasn't totally convinced Chad hadn't flipped and become a double-*double* agent until Chad lifted his pant leg to show off the microphone.

Why Chad?

Because he was perfect. If anyone could sound as if he were only looking out for himself, it was Chad. Chad was Harry Templeton's weak spot. That was the way Kyle had it figured. He figured if Chad saw himself in Harry Templeton, then Harry Templeton would see himself in Chad. In other words, Harry Templeton would never have searched Chad for a hidden microphone because it would have been pretty much like Harry Templeton searching himself.

"I never did like kids."

This was Harry Templeton. These were the first and last words he said after hearing his voice boomerang back at him and seeing Chad's hidden microphone and realizing his (Harry Templeton's) reign as the king of the biology world had just exploded in his face. Harry Templeton simply squared his shoulders, lifted his chin, and marched himself out of the mezzanine, down the stairs, and out the museum's revolving front door. He didn't glance at the hooting crowd. He didn't flinch when a taxi driver refused to unlock the passenger door. Everything about Harry Templeton's demeanor seemed to say that being exposed as a scoundrel and a thief was a minor inconvenience, like something you'd scrape off the sole of your shoe.

Would Lucinda's mom eventually press charges?

No.

Would Harry Templeton publicly apologize?

Don't be silly.

For the rest of his life, Harry Templeton may have been known as "The Biology Thief," but he seemed to embrace this new name like a medal of honor. In fact, the straight-to-cable movie based on his autobiography, *My Life as a Liar,* may have brought him nothing but hisses and boos when he appeared on television talk shows, but Harry Templeton seemed to bask in all these negative vibes. Who's to say how he really felt? Not anyone I know. Nor anyone Harry Templeton knew either, since he never got to know anyone ever again. People kept their distance. Even at Serendipity. Where rumor had it that every year on the first day of spring, this old guy with this paper-thin mustache sat at the table under that crazy grandfather clock and dumped a frozen hot chocolate all over his herringbone sports coat.

But that's it.

Finished.

Enough about Harry Templeton.

What mattered the most here was Lucinda's mom. And since she'd already waited twenty-three years for this moment, let's not let her wait any longer. Turns out she wouldn't have to. Because those initial wide-eyed gasps that ricocheted around that whale room over Harry Templeton's treachery quickly switched to kisses and hugs and congratulations all around as Loretta Winston's coronation and coming-out party kicked off with a serenade.

Oh, come on!

Don't act surprised!

After all, there *was* a crowd *and* a microphone. No way was Tyrone going to pass up an opportunity like this. Even before Lucinda's dad had a chance to propose the first toast, Tyrone was up at the podium. No backup singers. No piano to provide the tune. It was just Tyrone and a voice so haunting it could tear your heart in two on the very first note.

Only this wasn't a tragedy.

Tyrone wasn't singing opera.

He sang the song Lucinda had told him was her mom's favorite. He sang "Someone to Watch Over Me." And every word reminded Professor Winston how her daughter (and Kyle and the rest of the secret agents) had just watched over her big-time. And right there under that blue whale in front of all of those well-wishers, Lucinda's mom broke down and cried. Which made Lucinda cry. Which made her dad . . . Well, you get the picture. Things were on the verge of turning so emotional that any moment *Chad* might have started blubbering or hugging Tyrone or pulling some other stunt that would have haunted our dreams for the rest of our lives if Percy Percerville hadn't appeared out of nowhere at the top of those zigzag stairs—his black cape flapping, his lunatic dog howling at his heels.

"*NOT* HER?" he thundered. "*NOT* CYNTHIA MARLOW? WE'VE BEEN HOODWINKED, SHAKESPEARE! THIS WOMAN IS MERELY TRYING TO CURE CANCER! SHE'S NOT A ROMANCE NOVELIST AT ALL!"

Don't worry.

There's no way we're going to end this story with Percy shouting and Shakespeare leaping on his hind legs and spinning in the air three hundred and sixty degrees.

We're leaving.

We're jumping ahead twenty-two hours and joining Lucinda and her mom in their living room on Twentieth Street, far from the glitter of the Museum of Natural History.

It was Sunday evening.

Six thirty on the dot.

And we're just in time to hear Lucinda ask, "How do you think you're going to like being the head of NYU's biology department?" and Lucinda's mom answer, "Too much paperwork." And for those of us who think Lucinda's mom's attitude was pretty much like getting an A on a chemistry test then complaining it wasn't an A+, maybe we'd better take a closer look.

First off, Lucinda and her mom were sitting next to

each other on the couch. Second off, Lucinda's mom's bare foot was tickling Lucinda's bare foot in a way that only a mom can tickle her child's bare foot. No. I take that back. Lucinda's mom was tickling Lucinda's foot in a way that only a mom who isn't frightened or depressed or feeling guilty can tickle her child's bare foot. And, third off, Lucinda's cell phone was about to ring. And Lucinda's mom was about to kiss Lucinda on the cheek and say, "Tell them both hello for me." And thirty minutes later Lucinda and Kyle would be stepping back onto that tramway headed for Roosevelt Island to visit John T. Beecham and thank him for helping them fool Harry Templeton.

Was the subway tunnel still blocked?

Nope.

Was Kyle shaking again?

Yep.

Only this time it was Kyle who insisted they get off the F train at Sixty-third Street then quick-marched toward the East River—a turn of events some of us might call strange. Especially Lucinda. Especially since Kyle's only response to her repeated question of why they didn't simply stay on the subway was to answer, "You'll see when we get there." Which, as you might imagine, intrigued Lucinda to such a point that when that tramway door finally closed behind her she spread her feet and put her hands on her hips and jutted her chin out and looked Kyle dead in the eye.

"Okay," she said. "You got me here again, but I'm not taking another step until you tell me how come?"

"Because I chickened out the first time," Kyle said.

"No, you didn't. You rode the tram over to the island just like you're doing right now."

"That's not what I'm talking about."

"So what *are* you talking about?"

But Kyle still didn't answer.

Not out loud, at least.

Instead, he leaned in.

Closer . . .

Closer . . .

So close his lips brushed against Lucinda's lips. You heard me. Right there on that New York City tramway—with the conductor in her conductor's hat staring out the side window at the barge in the East River heading south and the other five passengers staring out the back window at the sun setting behind the Empire State Building—Kyle Parker was kissing Lucinda Winston for the first time.